D0870154

LIFE OF A COUNTERFEITER

AND OTHER STORIES

YASUSHI INOUE

LIFE OF A COUNTERFEITER

AND OTHER STORIES

Selected and translated by
Michael Emmerich

PUSHKIN PRESS
LONDON

Pushkin Press
71–75 Shelton Street, London WC2H 9JQ

'Life of a Counterfeiter', 'Reeds' and 'Mr. Goodall's Gloves' originally
published as ある偽作家の生涯 (*Aru gisakka no shōgai*, 1951),
蘆 (*Ashi*, 1956) and グウドル氏の手套 (*Gūdoru-
shi no tebukuro*, 1953) in Japan.

This translation is based on the text in *Inoue Yasushi zenshū*
(*Collected Works of Yasushi Inoue*), Tokyo, Shinchōsha (1995–1997).

This translation first published by Pushkin Press in 2014

ISBN 978 1 782270 02 7

Frontispiece: *Yasushi Inoue*, reproduced with
permission of The Wylie Agency

Set in 10 on 15 Monotype Baskerville
by Tetragon, London

Proudly printed and bound in Great Britain
by TJ International, Padstow, Cornwall
on Munken Premium White 90gsm

www.pushkinpress.com

CONTENTS

LIFE OF A
COUNTERFEITER

NEARLY A DECADE has passed since the Ōnuki family first asked me to compile a biography of the painter Ōnuki Keigaku, and I have yet to complete it. This spring, I received a printed announcement from the house in Kyoto saying they would be marking the thirteenth anniversary of Keigaku's death with a memorial service at a Zen temple; a postcard was enclosed, self-addressed and stamped, by which I was to inform them whether or not I would be able to attend. I must admit I was somewhat diffident about presenting myself to the family. For better or worse, work would make it impossible for me to participate in the ceremony anyway, but in all honesty it came as a relief that this was the case—I felt as if I had been saved.

It was in 1942, as I recall, that Takuhiko, the new head of the family, first contacted me to discuss the terms under which I might undertake to assemble Keigaku's biography; he indicated that, while the family was in no great hurry, they intended to present the book to the deceased on the seventh anniversary of his death, and to distribute copies at the ceremony, so they would be glad if I could finish the manuscript in time for it to be published by then. In the event, the seventh anniversary fell in March 1945, when the war was in its final stages, and both the Ōnuki family and I were in such frantic straits that the biography was nowhere in our thoughts; I had no choice but to put a temporary hold on my work while I was still gathering materials, and our agreement dissolved of its own accord. After the fighting ceased, however, the family approached me once again. Now that we were living in a more settled age, they said, the project could no longer be allowed to languish, and they desired that I might see it to completion in due haste. Ever since, perhaps once a year, I receive a postcard from Takuhiko inquiring, with a subtlety and delicacy so typical of him, how the biography is coming along; and each time I have replied with some tortuous excuse, buying a temporary reprieve.

I was chosen for the rather irksome task of preparing Keigaku's biography, it seems, because I had interviewed the deceased on a few occasions in my capacity as an arts reporter for an Osaka newspaper, which is what I was in those days, and he had liked me better than reporters from the other papers: this familiarity would make it relatively easy for me to collect materials. My position in the newspaper and the passing acquaintance with the painting community it had given me appears to have impressed both the Ōnuki family and Keigaku's disciples favorably as well, leading them to settle upon me as the person best suited to the job.

My decision to accept the commission—which I did with alacrity—was prompted in the first place by my admiration both for Ōnuki Keigaku the man and for his works; but also, and more importantly, by the realization that, in order to compile such a biography, I would essentially have to write a history of the entire Kyoto painting establishment, or indeed of painting at the national level. This would not be such a bad way, I thought, for a reporter who was supposedly a specialist in the arts to learn a bit about how painting had changed and evolved in this country since the Meiji period.

Having taken on the job in this rather cavalier manner, I discovered that the work itself was by no means as straight-forward as I had expected. I began by trying to piece together a timeline of Keigaku's life, only to find that until he built the magnificent estate in Kyoto where he lived out his final years he had been constantly on the move, bumping about from place to place as the spirit moved him—he had lived in more than ten houses just within Kyoto and its suburbs—and as if that weren't enough, he had spent almost half of each year traveling. It was all but impossible, then, to determine with any accuracy when and in which atelier he had painted even his greatest, most acclaimed works. In order to trace the sixty-odd years of his career, I had to piece together what I could learn from a number of disciples and fellow painters, as well as art dealers, framers, collectors, and so on—and each of their accounts conflicted with the others. Making a timeline was not as neat a task as it might appear from the outside.

Keigaku had lost his wife of many years, Mitsu, when he was fifty, and lived out the remainder of his life in a household of three, accompanied by an elderly maid who passed away two years after him and a series of students who did chores around the house in exchange for lodging. Keigaku was such a prickly man that none of the students stayed for long; one was always leaving, and another coming to take his place. Takuhiko, whom as heir one would have expected to be most knowledgeable about the deceased's doings, had spent many years in France, and although he had returned five years prior to Keigaku's death, he had his own house in Tokyo and had been so characteristically self-centered in his dealings with his father that he had essentially no experience of Keigaku's day-to-day life. The end result was that there was almost no one I could go to for detailed knowledge about Keigaku's private existence. And there was one more factor that placed hurdle after hurdle in my way as I attempted to gather materials for my biography, causing me no end of trouble: owing to his untamed personality, his wild disregard for matters that concerned more ordinary people, he had always been utterly indifferent to the painting establishment, and thus from start to finish remained isolated, a member of no school but his own.

In short, for all these reasons, I made hardly any progress at all, even on the timeline that should have been the foundation of my biography, managing to fill at best two or three notebooks by visiting towns near his birthplace, up and down the coast of the Inland Sea, where I saw his very first efforts, and by making trips to view the major later-period "decorative works," painted for selling, in the small weaving towns in the Hokuriku region where, oddly enough, many of his admirers were concentrated. And then, as the war escalated, my work on the biography came to an abrupt end, the basic research still only half done.

After the war, my feelings came to be dominated by an odd reluctance to embark again on a once-failed project, and while I knew I had no choice, insofar as I had taken the job, my acute awareness of the particular annoyances I would face made it hard to pick myself up and do what had to be done. What's more, when the war ended, I had—quite out of the blue, even from my own vantage—quit my post at the newspaper, moved to Tokyo, and plowed headfirst into the world of literature, so that all my time was occupied by writing of that nature; thus, what with this and that, I allowed my work on the biography to languish, putting it off until tomorrow, then the next day, with the result that even now, after all these years, I have yet to produce anything beyond that incomplete timeline, littered with blanks, and two or three notebooks of fragmentary jottings.

So the situation stood. The realization that I had now failed to produce the biography in time for even the thirteenth anniversary of Keigaku's death made me feel so ashamed of myself and my endless procrastinating, with respect both to the Ōnuki family and to the deceased himself, that I really could not have faced them; and so, ever since I received the announcement, I began to think that this year, at last, I absolutely had to cobble together at least the semblance of a biography, so that I would at least have half carried out my responsibility, and be free of that burden.

Since I knew from past experience that I never made much progress on my own work in July and August anyway, when the heat is at its worst, I arranged to devote these two months to the Keigaku biography, renting a small studio in

16

a village at the foot of Mt. Amagi, in Izu, where I was born and raised. I threw myself somewhat aggressively into the project, deciding to spend only mornings on it, and that I would simply leave anything I was uncertain of until the autumn, when I would make a trip to Kyoto to fill in the gaps; thus I would at least be able to finish the manuscript.

Work progressed smoothly enough in July: I went through nearly ten collections of Keigaku's occasional essays and travel writings and listed as many of his trips as I could identify, then added in his major works by year of composition—and with that I was able to complete a timeline of sorts, however slapdash. In August, relying on my old notes and trying as much as possible to set out only trustworthy facts, avoiding any speculation, I finished the section of the biography covering from his childhood through his teenage years, then wrote of his apprenticeships with a series of Kyoto painters, including Katakura Issō and Yoshimizu Gahō; the submission of his first important work, *Pleasures Lost*, to the 1897 Exhibition for the Promotion of Painting, and the really quite extraordinary splash with which his career began when the painting received an award, marking him as a genius from the beginning; and then, finally, his unveiling, in quick succession, of the works now regarded as his early masterpieces, among them *White Nights*, *The Old*

Fox, and *A Thin Layer of Snow*. After that, however, I suddenly found myself unable to write another word.

Here and there, in the course of describing Keigaku's glorious beginnings as a young artist, I had been transcribing sections from what was essentially the only holographic document to have survived, an unpublished diary from that period in his life that Ōnuki Takuhiko had handed me the first time I visited him in Kyoto after the war.

"I came across something unusual," he had said. "I wonder if you might find it useful?"

The diary contained scattered notes about day-to-day events from the end of 1897 to the summer of 1899, all written out in spidery characters on handmade Japanese paper; it was a precious, absolutely unique record of Keigaku's life during that period. Evidently the family had found it in a Chinese chest in the storehouse, mixed in with all sorts of other old papers, while they were preparing to evacuate.

The thing in this diary that most piqued my curiosity was the revelation that this brilliant, arrogant and haughty painter, who seemed never in his life to have possessed a true friend, had in fact been close to someone in those years—a man named Shinozaki. His name appeared three times. What was more, his was the only name in the diary's pages that did not belong to a family member. One entry read, "Went to see Shinozaki in Kitano with my silver medal; we spent the night drinking and talking." Judging from the context, this almost certainly occurred after Keigaku received the Special Award for *Picture of a Peacock* at the exhibition of the Kyoto Painting Association. Presumably he went to share his delight with his close friend, taking the medal with him, and the two had stayed up all night pouring each other cup after cup of sake; one can easily imagine that this must have been the happiest night in Keigaku's young life. That he was able to share his joy with Shinozaki so completely, without holding back, suggests that they must have been very close indeed.

The next entry reads: "Shinozaki sent a sea bream to congratulate me. Went right away to see him in Shimotachiuri, but he was out. Left a note, enormous, on the door to his room." Presumably Shinozaki had sent the sea bream because Keigaku had taken another prize at an exhibition or something like that; Keigaku, touched by this warm gesture, had immediately dashed off to Shinozaki's house, or perhaps to the room he rented. We have no way of knowing what the "enormous" note Keigaku left "on the door to his room" might have said, but in all likelihood it was either a note explaining the reason for his visit or a

19

poem in Chinese of the sort he often composed later in his life, spontaneously tossed off, expressing his gratitude for the gift. This was an extraordinarily reckless thing for Keigaku to do, but I found it fascinating—it seemed so perfectly to capture the proud confidence of a young, brilliant painter whose talents were only just being recognized. No date is given for this entry.

Shinozaki's name appears for the last time in this sentence: "Shinozaki left Mt. Shō this morning, came to Kyoto." This comes toward the end of the diary, in an entry dated August 3, 1899. The line has been written in on its own; it has no connection to what precedes or follows, and does not seem to have any particular meaning. And yet, the second I saw the two characters for Mt. Shō, an image rose up before me, perfectly clear, of that intimate friend of Keigaku's, the man he called Shinozaki: all of a sudden, I realized that he was the counterfeiter Hara Hōsen.

I had some slight knowledge of Hōsen as a man who had produced counterfeits of Keigaku's work and lived a dark, unhappy life, though until then I had half forgotten his existence. And yet, when it struck me that he must have been essentially the only close friend Keigaku ever had in his youth, I was struck by an emotion unlike anything I had ever felt, and that I don't know how to describe.

Casting my thoughts back, I realized I had once heard that Hōsen had been adopted, and, although I had never been told his original surname, the name Shinozaki was, it occurred to me, very common in the small settlement along the Hino river, in the Chūgoku mountains, where Hōsen had grown up. There could be no doubt, as far as I was concerned, that the Shinozaki who appeared in the diary and Hara Hōsen were one and the same.

For the next two days, I left my work on the biography and did nothing but sit in the rattan chair on my south-facing veranda, staring at Mt. Amagi and the late-summer sun, suddenly so much weaker than before, glowing on its slopes. My thoughts were occupied, not by the figure of that brilliant painter Keigaku in the full glory of his youth, but by Hōsen's checkered career—though obviously the little bits and pieces of knowledge I had concerning him were only then, for the first time, drawing together to form a single coherent thread, an image of a life. As I sat facing the mountain, a powerful urge came over me: I had to keep thinking about Hōsen. There was something in his life, it seemed, that I could not avoid thinking about—that I had, for his sake, to reflect upon.

*

I first encountered Hara Hōsen's name in the autumn of 1943 when Ōnuki Takuhiko and I took a trip together, thinking we should go look at a number of Keigaku's representative early works that remained scattered about in various towns on the Inland Sea, along the southern edges of Hyōgo and Okayama prefectures, owing to their proximity to Keigaku's hometown.

We gave ourselves about five days and visited the houses of owners of Keigaku's works in Akashi, Kakogawa, Takasago, Himeji, Shikama, Aioi, Wake and Saidaiji. Takuhiko had contacted someone at each house in advance to explain our motivation for coming; in most cases they welcomed us warmly, and we were able to see a number of paintings Keigaku had done in his twenties of which previously we had only heard.

We were kept quite busy getting on and off trains, stepping out onto the platforms of small stations in Harima and Bizen, where one could somehow intuit the nearness of the ocean and where the autumn sunlight splashed across the whitish, sandy soil characteristic of the region, and then making the rounds of the addresses I had copied out in my notebook, going from the house of one venerable or at least inordinately wealthy family to the next, each one of which had been a patron of Keigaku's, so to speak, while he was alive. Sometimes our schedule allowed us to stay no more than an hour or two, and even had that not been the case Takuhiko was innately given to rushing about, so I found myself hurrying, indeed almost sprinting, down long roads enclosed by pines or streets bordered by endless mud walls, but it was late autumn and I didn't sweat much at all—the weather was neither too hot nor too cold, ideal for a trip of this nature.

My primary purpose in coming on this trip was to view the paintings, but Takuhiko seemed to see it as an occasion to thank these families for throwing their weight behind his father during his life. At each house, we would hear an anecdote or two about the young Keigaku; sometimes, if the title of one of the scrolls in a collection hadn't been marked on its box, Takuhiko would be asked to take up a brush and write it in his own calligraphy, along with his father's name. "All right," he would say, an expression settling onto his face—under those bushy eyebrows, his close-cropped hair—that displayed a competitiveness he had inherited from his father, "let's have a go." And with that he would roll up his sleeves, baring arms that seemed too sturdy for a man who claimed to have set Paris on fire with rumors of his exploits, and write the characters in a style startlingly similar to Keigaku's.

I had hit it off unusually well with Takuhiko, who was my age and now well established as the second artist in Keigaku's family, and we had quickly grown friendly enough to speak quite candidly with each other. Takuhiko had lived such a thoroughly debauched life abroad that when he came back to Japan it felt ridiculous to go on that way, and just like that he reinvented himself, ceasing to bother about appearances or reputation, acquiring the air of a man from some far-off country casting cynical sideways glances at the chaotic goings-on of wartime Japan. He combined a haughty, audacious streak predictable in the son of a genius with the cheerful affability of a man from a good family. The reports I had heard before we met were so off the mark I hardly knew what to think; being the successor to a celebrated painter had, it seemed, subjected him to misunderstandings on every front.

Although Takuhiko had inherited a remarkable artistic talent from his father, he had a reputation as a lazy good-for-nothing, and, even though there was nothing at all stylish about him, no tendency to posture, rumor had it that he was a foppish playboy. Of course, he had inherited enormous wealth upon his father's death, along with a magnificent estate and a vacation house, so while I suppose you could have described him as a sculptor by trade, in actuality he didn't do anything, and didn't need to. Essentially the only tasks on his plate were to put out his father's biography before Japan finally lost the war, and then maybe publish a luxurious catalog of Keigaku's works.

In the course of our five-day trip together, Takuhiko and I encountered something quite intriguing that neither of us had expected. Every house we visited had, it turned out, a painting—and usually only one—that purported to be Keigaku's, but was in fact a forgery. We came across these works with such regularity it almost seemed the families must have gotten together and planned it.

The first was at the house of the wealthy M. family in Kakogawa, whose head had already died.

They showed us several of Keigaku's paintings in an inner room that looked out onto a carefully tended enclosed garden. Among them was one small scroll whose box bore the title "Autumn Scene, North of the Capital," evidently meant for use in the tea ceremony. I spotted it as a forgery as soon as it was unrolled, and Takuhiko, who had been peering down at it from the side, immediately glanced up at me, so that our gazes unexpectedly collided, and clung together for a moment.

"What do you think?" his eyes were saying.

I had seen exactly the same painting at the house of a collector in Kyoto, but Takuhiko could tell right away, even

25

without referencing such external circumstances, as he later explained, simply because there was a certain lack of grace in the execution. At any rate, the work had obviously been copied from a photograph in a catalog or some such thing. Just in case, we checked the manual of Keigaku's seals, and sure enough the one on this scroll was unmistakably a copy, evidently carved from wood, of the original stone "Tekishintei" seal. At first glance it appeared to be quite skillfully done, but when we lined the two marks up side by side the discrepancies were clear. The vermilion ink was a different shade, as well, and while the box had a title on it, as it should, the calligraphy was fake.

When we asked about the painting, the widow of the house told us her late husband had bought it from a painter named Hara Hōsen, a friend of Keigaku's who had temporarily taken up residence in Kakogawa and had gone around with a number of old pieces; she herself had been acquainted with the man, though she had no idea what had become of him.

"Ah, Hara Hōsen!" Takuhiko said when he heard this. "I know him, too, actually. I'm not entirely sure when it might have been, but I remember meeting him two or three times as a boy. It's true he was a friend of my father's, and he used to come over fairly often, but from what I've heard he made forgeries of my dad's paintings at some point, and after that my dad refused to see him. Seems the story was true."

This experience with the M. family in Kakogawa turned out to be only the beginning; at one house after the next, day after day, we were shown Keigakus painted by Hara Hōsen.

"Another Hōsen, huh?"

"This one's quite good, actually—almost better than the real thing."

Each time, after exchanging a few remarks of this sort, we would inform the unfortunate owners that the piece was a counterfeit. In some cases we could tell at a glance that the painting was fake, but some of the imitations were surprisingly skillful. Still, they could be clearly distinguished from originals by their lack of a certain innate quality, or by their less commanding aura—they were fakes, after all—and upon careful examination there was always some blatant mistake.

From his middle period on, Keigaku abandoned the use of short, pale-green lines in depicting the surfaces of boulders, grass or moss, and so sometimes one could instantly point to an error of this sort; in other cases, Keigaku's unusual technique of applying azure blue near the bottom of the snow in paintings of Mt. Fuji in the summer—a favorite theme of his—had been so sloppily

27

mimicked that it could be cited as evidence of a fake. In every instance, without exception, the counterfeits revealed themselves.

That Hōsen was responsible for all these forgeries was evident from the routes by which they had been acquired. He must have been an exceptionally adroit man, because in the large majority of cases he seemed not only to have painted the work, but also to have prepared the different seals and even done the calligraphy on the box; indeed, of the dozen or so forgeries we saw during our trip, only two appeared to have been sold in partnership with sketchy country art dealers.

There was a reason for this: in his interactions with buyers, Hōsen had usually invoked his friendship with Keigaku as his trump card, using this to gain their trust before telling them he had received a certain painting as a gift from Keigaku, or bought it for very little, and then pushing the forgery onto them. On other occasions, Hōsen would offer to ask Keigaku to do a painting for the buyer, and then, after waiting for a plausible amount time, he would bring the painting along.

As I noted, only two works had come to their buyers through an unscrupulous, unidentified dealer. Still, this indicated that at some point Hōsen had indeed partnered with such a person to sell his forgeries, and that made the whole business even more serious.

During our trip, Takuhiko and I took to calling the counterfeiter by different names: "Hara Keigaku," "old man Hara," and so on. We had the opportunity to inspect a dozen or so of his counterfeits, and gleaned scraps of knowledge about the man from talking with their owners, but the stories we heard all dated from when he was in his forties and fifties, from the period when he had lived in the area, roving from place to place as an unknown local painter; the most we could do to satisfy our curiosity about the extent of his friendship with the young Keigaku was to speculate on the basis of Takuhiko's hazy memories.

Piecing together what we learned from the victims onto whom Hōsen had unloaded his forgeries, we determined that he had lived for some time in each of the small coastal cities we had visited—three years in Aioi, two in Shikama, four in Wake, and so on—but that he had never settled in any one place for as much as five years. Given that he was the sort of man to go about selling counterfeits, I suspect that after two or three years some incident would make it impossible for him to remain in each town, leaving him no choice but to move. Presumably he went on hopping from one small city to the next one in the vicinity, rather than picking up and leaving for someplace farther away, because he would have been unable to earn a living outside this region so rich in collectors of Keigaku's work.

S., the president of a sake distillery in Wake, was the only person to whom Hōsen had introduced his wife. For whatever reason, Hōsen had brought the petite but beautiful woman to this man's house not once but on many occasions; according to what we were told, Hōsen had gained the confidence of the previous head of the household to quite an extraordinary degree.

"I have the impression Hōsen was less a painter himself than a sort of dealer. I was still a child at the time, so my memory isn't very clear, but I believe my father often relied on Hōsen when he wanted to commission a work from a painter in Tokyo, for example. Most of the paintings in this house came to us through him, I'd say."

The present head of the household, who told us this, was in his forties—he had been a celebrated rugby player in college, and didn't look as though he had much interest in paintings.

He continued: "I had the sense he was good at everything. He even carved his own seals, you know. I think we have one he did around here somewhere."

The man looked for the seal, but couldn't recall where they kept it.

We asked him to show us a few of the paintings by famous Tokyo artists his father had acquired through Hōsen, but they were all absolutely authentic; one was such a remarkably accomplished piece, though it was small, that it was surprising the artist had been willing to send it off to a place like this, way out in the country. Whatever Hōsen's failings may have been, Tokyo's painters seemed to have placed a good deal of trust in him.

"So Hōsen specialized in Keigaku," Takuhiko said. "And he navigated very cautiously, never selling two counterfeits to the same family."

It was true. Hōsen had been very clever, and very careful.

According to our researches, Kakogawa was the only place Hōsen had lived in twice—though we couldn't say why. He would have been in his late fifties the second time, which lasted from 1927 to 1928; after that he had left the region behind. Or rather, he didn't necessarily leave; he simply stopped turning up, around that time, at the houses of the local art lovers.

On the fifth and final day of our travels, on the way back from Saidaiji, we took a room in a small, well-known inn in Himeji, near the shore. We intended to relax a little, eat some fresh fish, and divest ourselves of the weariness of five days of travel. By some amazing coincidence, however, we discovered a landscape by Hōsen hanging in the alcove of our room. The first seal, in a style close to block script, was easily legible as "Hōsen"; the second and third read "Kankotei" and, once again, "Hōsen."

Owing in part, perhaps, to our weariness after so much traveling, this odd encounter with Hōsen's work seemed inordinately funny.

"Some strange karma seems to bind us to the great painter," Takuhiko said. "And look here, he's taken off the mask on this one. Surely it's not a counterfeit of his own work!"

We remained there, still standing, cracking jokes and gazing at the scroll in the alcove. We had seen several of Hōsen's counterfeit Keigakus, of course, but this was the first time we had encountered a work of his own, signed with his own name.

"Not half bad, is it?" Takuhiko said, looking a bit taken aback. "He could have made non-vetted status at the Ministry of Education Exhibit, I'd say."

At the very least, it wasn't the sort of anonymous garbage one often finds hanging in the alcove of your average inn. The subject matter was trite—part of a mountain shrouded in mist, painted in the Nanga style—but it was executed with such exquisite attention to detail that one could see why Hōsen had signed it with his own name. In some strange fashion, I felt the scene burrowing its way into my heart as I stood gazing at it.

"Odd spirit in there," Takuhiko said.

And it was true: something in the painting called for such a description. No one who had just seen a sampling of Keigaku's masterpieces could regard it as a genuinely superior work, but its peculiarly solitary, impoverished spirit gave it a certain attractive harshness.

"Kankotei. 'Pavilion of Cold Antiquity.' A perfect name for an artist," Takuhiko said, evidently profoundly moved; then, having inspected the painting once more, he went out to the veranda and sat down on one of the rattan chairs. As he went, the sound of the name he had just uttered, *Kankotei*, was finding its chill way into the recesses of my own heart, and I had to agree that in some odd way it exactly matched the mood of the painting.

We spent the evening—the last of our trip—sharing a few small bottles of sake. We tended to grow most enthusiastic when the conversation turned to Hara Hōsen, rather than during our discussions of the early masterpieces of Keigaku's we had spent the past week investigating.

The conclusion we reached was that Hōsen must have had some degree of talent, given that he was capable of paintings as good, despite their problems, as those we had seen.

"What a fool. He should have painted his own works, rather than wasting his time making stupid knock-offs of my father's!"

Casting a sideways glance at the scroll in the alcove, Takuhiko pushed up the sleeves of the thin cotton yukata the inn had provided and raised his cup to his lips.

"I'm sure the counterfeits sold better."

"That's true. People would go for a Tekishintei over a Kankotei."

"What kind of a man was he, I wonder? You have no memory of him?"

I felt a certain curiosity about this charlatan, the impression he had made.

"None at all. I was just a boy, after all, and besides, the most I would have done is catch a glimpse of him in the entryway or something. I suppose there was one time, come to think of it, when my dad was about forty, I'd say, because I must have been seven or eight…"

Takuhiko recounted his most deeply memorable encounter with Hōsen.

He had no idea where it had happened, but presumably it was an exhibition. Hōsen was kneeling on the floor with his head bowed to the floor while Keigaku towered over him.

"Lift your head and look me in the eye!"

Takuhiko had, he said, a faint memory of his father shouting these words. Keigaku was livid, he kept shouting, repeating himself, but no matter what he said Hōsen never raised his head. Takuhiko had no impression of Hōsen's appearance, what sort of air he possessed, but he remembered feeling deeply sorry for the man, even though he was too young to understand.

"My dad must have found out about the forgeries, and… well, you know what he was like—he didn't care, he'd fly off the handle even in front of other people. We weren't at home, so it must have been one of my dad's exhibitions, at some department store or museum, maybe a temple, and my dad must have caught him there. Something along those lines, I'm sure. My dad might have been helping him out financially then, too. Sounds like an old ballad the way I tell it."

Takuhiko treated it as a joke, but Keigaku seems to have given Hōsen money more than just once or twice. Takuhiko remembered hearing this from his father and mother, and the faint recollections that came when he cast his thoughts back to the two other times he had seen Hōsen, if that's who it was, suggested that the man had either come to borrow money, or been summoned for a scolding by his father—something like that, in any event, must have been responsible for the way Hōsen hung his head when he left, judging from the mood of the scenes Takuhiko had peeked in on.

"That time I saw him prostrating himself, unable to look up—I don't think he ever appeared in my father's presence again after that," Takuhiko said. "Once I started middle school, I never heard my old man mention him visiting, and when he did talk about him it was always in a very retrospective sort of mode. 'I had this friend once, a real bad character…' That kind of thing."

We stayed up late that night, drinking before that painting of Hara Hōsen's, and then spread our futons out on the floor in front of it and went to sleep.

The second time I encountered Hara Hōsen's name was near the end of the war, in the spring of 1945, which makes it about a year and a half after Ōnuki Takuhiko and I went on our trip around the towns along the Inland Sea. During that period there had been a dramatic shift in the direction of the war, and the country had become almost unrecognizably gritty and desolate: people's day-to-day lives, their hearts, even nature itself had changed.

I had evacuated my mother, my ailing wife, and our two small children to a village near the ridge of the Chūgoku mountains, relying on the good graces of an acquaintance there of one of my colleagues at the paper. The place was about as isolated as it could be, located near the area where Okayama, Hiroshima and Tottori prefectures abutted each other and falling just within the borders of the last. No matter how the war ended, it was the sort of spot where life would keep rolling placidly along, day after day, just as it had since ancient times.

I went for a first visit to get a sense of the area, before shipping my family off in late March. The only person I had any connection with there—the acquaintance of my colleague upon whom I would be relying for help—was a man named Ogami Senzō.

The eight-kilometer road that led to the village from the station at the summit, on the Hakubi line, was incredibly steep, just barely wide enough for one person, and I had to cross two small peaks on the way; once I entered the village, though, the land was so level it was difficult to believe it was on a mountainside, and the view was wide open in every direction. The sunlight and the scent of the wind were totally different from down below. Fifty or so houses dotted the spacious plateau, and the whole settlement brimmed with a light so free from any shadows that it actually left me feeling a bit empty. For the first time, up there, I experienced the sensation of light raining down from the sky. A shallow river perhaps nine meters across ran down the center of the plateau; it was hard to tell at first glance which was upriver and which was downriver, though in fact it was flowing north.

Still in his farming clothes, Ogami took me to see the village Youth Center—a building hardly any different from the farmhouses, despite its name—which we had been told we could rent, and I decided immediately to take it. That night I stayed with the Ogamis. Every household in the village had done so well with its fields that you would have been hard pressed to find such wealthy farmers elsewhere: each family owned two or three cows, and their houses were built in an old, unfussy style. Evidently the Ogami family could trace its roots back further than any other in the village, and their house was a size bigger than the rest. The room where they let me sleep was separated from the storage area by a sliding door fashioned from a solid board of Japanese cypress.

And in this room, in the incongruously small half-mat alcove, I discovered a picture of Keigaku's: a fox beneath a peony, turning to look this way. I was startled to see it there. As wealthy as they were, this was hardly a picture one would expect to find in a farmhouse up in the mountains.

"That's quite a piece you have there," I said to Ogami. He was in his fifties, and looked like the last man you would expect to have anything to do with painting.

"Yes, I hear it isn't the kind of thing people like us can often get hold of..." For some reason, Ogami's deeply suntanned face, with its simple, rugged air, had taken on a bashful coloring. "Happens there was a fellow in the village who used to be his best friend," he said. "The painter's, I mean. It's a man named Keigaku who did it."

"What was this friend's name?" I asked.

"Hara Hōsen he was called. He was a painter, too. Died back in 1940, though, if memory serves. From these parts originally, and came back home at the end of his life."

I required no further explanation—everything was clear. I was surprised to learn that Hara Hōsen had come from this area, I must say. And even though he was a perfect stranger, hearing that he had died touched a certain chord in me, if only very faintly. Just one year after Keigaku had passed away, his counterfeiter, Hara Hōsen, had followed.

39

That evening, I wrote a letter to mail to Kyoto, where Ōnuki Takuhiko was no doubt fraying his nerves day and night, rushing to move the enormous collection of artworks his father had left behind out of the city. I told him that Hōsen was dead, and that by some strange trick of karma it looked as though my family would be evacuating to his hometown.

About a month later, I moved my family to the village. Deep-purple flowers were blooming on the akebia vines in the thicket behind the Youth Center, where the four all-but-helpless members of my family were to live. April was almost over, but the air was still chilly, and when I dipped my hand into the stream that ran past the house the water was as cold as in winter.

I spent about five days helping my family get settled in before returning to Osaka, and on one of those days I went to pay my respects at the house of the village head, whose family traced its roots in the area back almost as far as the Ogamis. In the reception room, I came across another of Hōsen's counterfeit Keigaku's—the second I had seen in the village. This one was a 240-centimeter picture of birds and flowers, and although it was a fake it was quite forceful.

Needless to say, I kept quiet about the pictures, revealing their secret neither to the Ogamis nor to the village head.

I had absolutely no desire to push unwanted information upon people who believed they owned a painting by
Keigaku at a time when the very survival of the nation was
in doubt. In all likelihood, their Hōsen–Keigaku forgeries
would never leave this mountaintop village; for hundreds
or perhaps even thousands of years, they would pass from
hand to hand, from one person who had never even heard
of Ōnuki Keigaku to the next. This wouldn't change, no
matter what became of the country, I thought. And all of
a sudden, I felt—though the feeling lasted only as long
as the thought—that I was in the presence of something
eternal. My distress as I prepared to entrust my family to
this unfamiliar place, in these times, plunging them into a
world of unknown feelings, unknown customs, had left me
feeling altogether different about those counterfeits than I
had a year and a half ago.

I visited the village three times to check on my family
between then and the conclusion of the war in August.
On the third of those trips, I think it was, I went to inspect
another empty farmhouse in the village for that same colleague at the paper, guided by the old, bent-over woman
who was looking after it. The house stood on a low rise
at the village's south end, where the land began sloping
gently up and down; apparently it was higher than any

of the others, and it was set apart from the settlement, all on its own. I was surprised to learn from the woman that this was where Hōsen had lived. Almost five years had passed since he died, but it had been left undisturbed, uninhabited.

The building was so dilapidated that I was hesitant even to go inside. The house hadn't originally been Hōsen's, but when he came back to the village the year of the Manchurian Incident he bought it for next to nothing. According to the old woman, Hōsen wasn't from this part of the village, but from another small settlement about four kilometers away; he didn't get along with his older brother, who had inherited his parents' house, so instead of returning to the area where he had grown up he took this house and settled down here.

"Where's his family?" I asked, puzzled that the house had been left empty after Hōsen's death.

"His wife, you mean? Oh, she ran away," the woman said nonchalantly.

"Ran away!?"

"Imagine she got fed up with him. She stayed with Old Hara some three years, and then she went back to her parents' house in Shōyama for the festival and didn't come back."

Hōsen had gone to fetch her, concerned neighbors had interceded, but in the end she refused to return. For some reason Hōsen had been adopted into his wife's family when they married, so in order for the couple to be formally divorced he would have had to remove himself from their family register; evidently that had never happened, but the long and the short of it was that from then on they were separated.

"Let me think if she came when he died... I believe she may have been here for the funeral, but she never came back once until then."

"How old is she?"

"Hara was sixty-seven or sixty-eight when he died, so she must be past sixty now, even if she was ten years younger than him," the old woman said. "I hear she lives with relatives in Shōyama."

It turned out, then, that Hōsen had come back to his hometown in his old age, and passed away in the village of his birth—and yet, as the old woman told it, it seemed just the sort of down-and-out ending one might expect of a counterfeiter, his last years deeply tinged with sorrow.

I stepped up into the wasted house without removing my straw sandals, and aimlessly opened the door of a cabinet that stood next to the sunken hearth. It was filled with junk, everything covered in dust and cobwebs. The old woman, who had poked her head in at the same time I did, plucked out a few dishes, commenting that they could still be used.

"Old Hara used them when he made fireworks," she explained. She wiped the dust away, then set them down just inside the door, on the step up from the dirt entryway into the house proper, evidently intending to take them when we left.

"Fireworks?" I asked.

"He made fireworks here."

She scraped around in the junk with a stick, knocking things out onto the torn tatami, telling me to look, all those things were tools for making fireworks. Mixed in among the dust as it rose were fine black particles like soot.

"They say there's gunpowder, that's why no one wants to clean it out."

So the old woman said, even as she went on blithely stirring the rubbish on the tatami with her stick. Three or four half-spheres, like halved rubber balls, jumped out of the pile, and it was true—traces of yellow powder adhered to each, down at the bottom, suggesting they may once have held gunpowder. All sorts of things lay scattered about: what seemed to be papier-mâché shells; torn paper bags leaking black powder; suspicious objects about the size and shape of medicine balls; hardened clumps of what must have been that same black powder; as well as paint dishes; calligraphy and painting brushes; spatulas; bundles of Japanese paper; a mortar.

I was somewhat taken aback to learn that Hōsen had been making fireworks. Stepping down into the earthen-floored room I found that it, too, was so littered with trash of the sort inside the cabinet, flecks of rice chaff mixed in among it, that there was hardly a place to stand. The chaff, the old woman explained, was something Hōsen had put in his fireworks.

"He used to sit over here to make them."

The old woman was in an area beyond the earthen-floored room that in most farmhouses would have served as a cowshed; even from the outside, I could sense how dark and gloomy a space it was. A wooden table and a stump that must have been his seat were the only indications amidst the mess that this had once been a workroom. A half-broken scale stood beside a few bottles on the sill of the small window that was the only light source; protective amulets had been pasted here and there on the decorative wooden panels above the sliding doors, guards against fire.

I had decided the second I set foot in the house that my friend couldn't evacuate his family here—cleaning the place up enough to make it habitable would be too much of an undertaking.

I stood for a time in the center of the impossibly cluttered earthen-floored room, my eyes fixed on the dark corner in the storeroom where Hōsen had made his fireworks. I had never met the man, the deceased, and I had no way of imagining his appearance, the impression he had made, but now, for the first time, a sort of image rose up in my mind's eye: I saw Hara Hōsen as something like a dull, apathetic beast, huddled there in the darkness.

He must have sat on his stump at the table, fiddling with the scale and the various powders—black, red, yellow. Bars of light stream in diagonally from outside, from behind. The surrounding air is dim, cold and still. My sense of Hōsen here, in this house, was darker and more miserable than my image of him as a counterfeiter.

There's something unpleasant here, I thought. And no sooner had I felt this than I recalled the strange spirit that brimmed in the ink painting Ōnuki Takuhiko and I had seen at the inn in Himeji. Whatever it was we had sensed in that work filled this eerie, vacant house as well, floor to ceiling—only here it took a dirtier, uglier form.

As we were leaving, we went around back and the old woman pointed out "Old Hara's grave" to me. Beyond a narrow patch of unused land was a drop of about four meters; the unremarkable rock she had indicated squatted, half buried in weeds, near the ledge. A vast, panoramic view spread out behind it. Mountain ridges undulated gently in the distance; dropping my gaze, I saw the village houses dotting the plateau, tiny as toys, each one shouldering a mass of foliage. It was July, but it didn't look like summer. The whole landscape felt as cold and settled as if it were underwater.

That evening, the extremely inarticulate Ogami Senzō recounted in some detail Hōsen's final years in the village.

As he told it, Hōsen and his wife Asa had returned the year of the Manchurian Incident, in winter, bringing with them essentially nothing but the clothes on their backs. While they had no real luggage to speak of, they did have a small sum of money, and they used this to purchase—for very little, it was true—what the villagers called "the house on the hill," which was standing empty, its former residents having died one after the other of tuberculosis. They paid the asking price, handing over the money and taking up residence right away.

Hōsen encouraged the village headman, the Ogamis, and one or two other families in the village to buy the paintings he claimed were Keigaku's shortly after he moved back. He had only visited once or twice in the years since he had declared he was going to be a painter and left the village in his late teens, so hardly anyone here was well acquainted with his character. Once, a long time ago, a rumor had reached the village that Hōsen had become a great artist in Kyoto and Osaka, and when he came up in conversation the villagers always treated him as a man who had gone off and made it in the world. They had been a bit surprised, accordingly, at his wretched appearance when he returned later in life. It seems Hōsen told the villagers he had contracted rheumatism in recent years: his right arm hurt too much for him to do anything as delicate as paint with a brush, and so once his savings ran dry he had come back to the village.

He didn't really do any work after he settled down. Every so often he would head off to Yonago, Okayama, Tottori, and so on, with scrolls and antiques, then return with new ones, so he must have gone on being a sort of dealer, if only on a small scale, even after he retired to the countryside.

Hōsen hadn't made a particularly bad impression on the villagers, and he never caused others any trouble, so early on they called him "Mr. Hōsen, Mr. Hōsen," imbuing the name with a certain degree of respect; over time, as his trips became less frequent, and then as it came to be known that he was fooling around with gunpowder, even taking sparklers he had made to sell to toy stores in Yonago, people started referring to him as "Old Hara" instead.

Needless to say, Hōsen wasn't a genuine fireworks maker; he made them illicitly. He seems to have been working with explosives from the time he moved to the village—once, late at night, the villagers had raised a ruckus when a ball of fire shot up into the sky over Hōsen's house, only to be stunned when they learned afterward that he had launched what was known as a "falling star."

In his third year in the village, Hōsen lost three of the fingers on his right hand when some of his gunpowder exploded. After this incident—in part because people were disgusted that he was handling such a nasty substance—his popularity plummeted. Hōsen himself grew oddly arrogant in the wake of the accident, as if he had been wronged somehow, and from then on he no longer tried to conceal what he was doing, and began making his fireworks almost openly.

For the most part the villagers kept their distance from Hōsen's house, but whenever they chanced to look in on him they would find him sitting in the former cowshed, now remade into a workspace, preparing various types of toy fireworks—evidently orders from Yonago or some such place.

Half a year or so after Hōsen lost his fingers, he and Asa separated. Even Ogami felt he couldn't just stand by and watch when that happened, so he played the middleman, going to meet with Asa at her parents' house in Shōyama to ask her to come back to Hōsen, but try as he might she never said anything but *I won't do it*. Two or three other neighbors took their turns going to Shōyama as well, but to no avail. In the end, Hōsen gave up on their relationship, seeing how deeply Asa wanted to be rid of him. The villagers didn't really hold it against Asa that she had abandoned her husband of so many years. His right hand, with its three missing fingers, was dreadful to look at, and when you stopped to think about it there was something so dismal in the image of him toying with his gunpowder in the dim workroom that you could see even his wife might get fed up.

Hōsen's finances improved somewhat once he started making fireworks, though since he was doing it illegally he couldn't be too open about it, and it seems he was quite liberal—even a bit too liberal—when the time came to make donations to village road projects, and in the customary monetary gifts neighbors made at weddings and funerals. Once the police came after him, and he was dragged off to the station in a nearby town, but he must have smooth-talked his way out somehow because he seemed not to have paid a fine, and he kept working on his fireworks in the dark workroom just as before.

In the end, Hōsen continued his solitary existence in the village for almost a decade, until his death in 1940. He must have gotten his hands on a smallish sum of money at some point, because while on extremely rare occasions someone would see him working on what appeared to be fireworks, for the most part he spent his last three years sitting on the veranda, or lying there, doing nothing but gaze off into space. Still, when summer came he would make the boys in the area as many fireworks as they wanted, accepting small payments in recompense. When pressed he would occasionally carry a load of his fireworks to a nearby village, where he would launch them for their summer festival or some similar event, so that people elsewhere came to regard him—"Old Hara," as they said—with greater affection than his own neighbors.

Hōsen's death came completely unexpectedly. One morning, when the rains that had been falling for ages finally let up, someone from a neighboring house, perhaps a hundred meters away, realized he hadn't seen Old Hara for two or three days, and when he went to check in on him he found him sprawled out face down in the earthen-floored room. Hōsen's body was cold enough that some hours must have passed since he died, and rigor mortis was setting in. He had died of a stroke.

The intriguing thing about Hōsen's death is that he was about to do a painting when it happened. He had spread two folded blankets on the floor of the storeroom, and neatly lined up a few dishes holding paints and, beside these, the box holding his inkstone with five painting brushes on its lid—their tips, too, precisely aligned. A single sheet of fresh white paper had been centered on the blankets, spread out so that there wasn't a wrinkle. He had not yet begun to paint.

Presumably Hōsen had gotten everything ready, then recalled something he needed to do and gone into the earthen-floored room, where he collapsed.

"Did Hōsen do any painting toward the end of his life?" I asked Ogami.

"No, I don't think he did," he said. "But he was a painter at heart, of course—I suppose he must have sensed death coming, and wanted to paint one last time. Anyway, I doubt he could have painted anything worth looking at with three fingers gone."

There was something touching in the story of Hōsen's death, even if he had been a counterfeiter. For some reason, I found myself thinking he hadn't really intended to paint a picture; that this wasn't what the sheet of paper lying there, unmarked by a single stroke of his brush, meant. It struck me that perhaps he had simply wanted to be surrounded by those painterly implements.

After Ogami had told me what he knew of Hōsen, as I was preparing to leave he suddenly had a thought. "Come to think of it," he said, "I believe there are some notes Old Hara wrote in one of the cabinets in your storeroom. About fireworks, I think. We came across them at the time of the funeral, and some of the young men put them away for safekeeping in the Youth Center, thinking they might come in handy sometime."

There was one cabinet in the storeroom of the house we were renting that we had agreed to leave untouched, just as it had been when the building was still a Youth Center. It held various items that the young men of the village held in common.

I opened the cabinet as soon as I got back. It was packed with all kinds of useless papers: records of festival donations, minutes of youth group meetings, manuscripts for speeches, that sort of thing. Among these scraps, however, was a hand-bound notebook made of *hanshi*-sized paper, on the cover of which was written, in skillful calligraphy, "The Essentials of Firework Preparation." The imposing title belied what appeared to be simply a collection of Hōsen's notes on the fireworks he had made. Turning to the first page, I found the title: "Misty Blossom—Red Mist—Snowfall."

> To make the star, first prepare a safflower core. When it has dried, mix clay with chrysanthemum powder, kneading thoroughly with water until soft, then cut and blend in approximately 1.5% of a magnesium stick, put the mixture in a bowl, and thoroughly coat the core. Once it is evenly covered, prepare a powder from 100 *monme* chrysanthemum and 10 *monme* seeds and sprinkle it all over, then roll into a ball. Repeat as necessary until the star is a good size, perhaps four or five *sun* across, then finish with a layer of bursting powder. Note, however, that it is necessary to sun-dry it completely after each application. Use a 4.55 or 6.3 *sun* core.

Extremely unclear directions of this nature had been written out over three pages, followed by entries giving the recipes for "safflower powder" and "chrysanthemum powder," with the required quantities of gunpowder for each marked in red ink. The remainder of the book contained entries on preparing "Crossette Comets," "Straight Bursts," "Double Leaves," and so on. Hōsen had intended these notes as memos to himself, of course, and since I knew nothing about fireworks it was all quite beyond me. A piece of *hanshi* paper that had been tucked between the pages, however, turned out, when I opened it up, to be Hōsen's résumé. This interested me greatly, though for reasons unrelated to the contents. I say this because, while the presence of Hōsen's birthday at the beginning—"Hara Senjirō (Hōsen), b. October 3, 1874"—unmistakably identified the résumé as Hōsen's own, the entries, transcribed in tiny characters, were obviously all fake. "1916–Arareya Fireworks Store, Tokyo; 1918–Suzuki Fireworks Emporium, Yokosuka; 1921–Overseer Tōyō Fireworks Factory; 1922–Sakai Fireworks Emporium, Osaka; 1924–Overseer Marudamaya Fireworks Factory, Osaka"—so they went. At the end of the list, Hōsen had added, in a rather ostentatious fashion: "With reference to the above, all this is confirmed as being free from error."

There was no way of knowing when and to whom Hōsen had intended to submit this résumé, but the years he had listed, all during the Taishō era, corresponded to the period when he had been roving around Hyōgo and Okayama prefectures, from one small city to the next, peddling his Keigaku counterfeits. Clearly, then, this résumé was a complete fabrication. Perhaps at some point, finding himself unable to make a living either from his forgeries or as a local painter, he had tried to find employment as the chief technician at some fireworks factory. One might go further and imagine that, when he was called in by the police that one time, he used this same fraudulent résumé to pull the wool over his questioners' eyes, and had managed as a result to escape unscathed.

At any rate, this piece of paper revealed in the plainest possible manner the essence of Hara Hōsen. Of this there could be no doubt.

"This isn't the sort of thing you would have any experience with, I'm sure, but the truth is it's extremely unpleasant working with gunpowder in winter… the niter gives you such a chill, so icy cold you can't even describe it."

Hara Hōsen's widow held her right hand out as she spoke, glancing at her palm as if it were a mirror, as if recalling how chapped her skin had been. This was the year the war ended, in late November.

Even now that the fighting was over, life in the city remained shrouded in tremendous uncertainty and confusion, and lately each day's newspaper carried another article about an armed raid, so until recently I had been planning to have my family stay in our house in the village until New Year's; the seasons turned a full month earlier there than elsewhere, though, and, by the end of September, dreary, desolate winds had begun barreling up the mountain slopes several times a day, forming a ferocious corridor of wind that blew straight through from Mimasaka to Hōki, and then in October the showers that are such a unique feature of winter in the mountains began sweeping past, one after another—the first indication that the coldest season was approaching.

Around this time, my wife seemed suddenly to have grown afraid of spending winter snowbound in an unfamiliar region, and when I went to visit in early October she informed me, out of the blue, that she wanted to leave as soon as possible. She wasn't sure she could see my elderly mother and our two children through winter here, without even a heater, and if the children were to catch pneumonia there would be no doctor to take them to… After I returned to Osaka, my wife kept harping on about the same points in every one of her letters, trying to persuade me that they should come back.

In the middle of November, I took a somewhat long vacation to go help my family move out of our mountain village in Tottori prefecture; by the time I had disposed of the assorted difficulties that arose in connection with having our things transported and shipped off and so on and had finally got all the arrangements made, bringing me at last to the point where I was ready to lead my family away, only a few days remained before the end of the month.

On the appointed date, I set out in the afternoon for the train station in Shōyama—a town whose name I had heard but which I had yet to visit—to ship our belongings home on the San'in line. I knew the station master at the next stop, the one at the summit where I always got on and off, and things would undoubtedly have gone much more smoothly if I could have sent everything off from there, but the route was made too difficult for a move by the peaks between the house and the station.

The various negotiations relating to our luggage at Shōyama Station ended up being less involved than I had expected: the man I spoke with told me that if I could wait until evening a truck would be going out to the village where we lived. Walking nearly eight kilometers of mountainous road for the second time in a day seemed like more trouble than I wanted to take, so I decided to hitch a ride on the truck instead.

As I was wondering how to kill the two hours left until then, I suddenly remembered hearing that Hōsen's widow lived here with her brother. I had no reason to visit the woman, I realized, but then it was always possible she might have some small anecdote to share that related, not so much to Hōsen himself, but to Ōnuki Keigaku, about whom I would eventually have to write my biography, and so I decided to go and see her after all, in part as a way to pass the time.

I managed to track down Hōsen's wife right away by asking at the general store outside the station. Until two or three years ago the woman, Asa, had run a small candy shop across the way, but as the war escalated she ran out of sweets to sell and decided to close it; she wasn't working now, and relied for her food and lodging on the generosity of her elder brother, who had a lumber yard or some such thing. So I was told. And so it came about that I went and met Asa on the veranda of a house with quite an imposing demeanor, though I doubted the family had much money.

Naturally I had no way of discerning whether it was a blessing or a misfortune for her to be living with her brother's family, but she was neatly dressed; she sat on the narrow veranda, basking in the late afternoon sun, peeling persimmons with a kitchen knife, presumably to hang from the eaves to dry. The owner of the sake distillery in Wake had described her, long ago, as petite but beautiful, and it was true: you could tell she had been gorgeous when she was young, and even now there was a cool, sophisticated

59

sort of briskness in both her speech and her bearing that reminded me of the women you find at clubs or restaurants, and seemed unexpected in a women now in her sixties. And yet when she turned her head to the side, I was struck by the thinness of her earlobes, which gave an impression of poverty, and suggested, somehow, that her life had not in fact been happy. I had expected that she might decline to talk about Hōsen, since he had lived and died as a fraud, a painter of counterfeits, but she gave no indication that this was the case.

"I believe when he was young he was friends with Master Keigaku, but after I married him—well, I suppose he may have gone to see the Master at his house in Hyakumanben when he visited Kyoto, but their relationship wasn't what you would call a friendship. After all, there was that unbelievable period in his life when he made those forgeries, so he couldn't face the man."

I was startled to see how clinically she spoke of him. On the face of it, she no longer let herself be troubled by her long-time husband's deplorable actions; all that belonged to the past.

"I separated from him in 1935. Between then and the time he died, he came to see me only once. That was the day the papers reported Master Keigaku's death."

Hōsen had come to ask her to attend Keigaku's funeral and light a stick of incense in his place, since he himself couldn't possibly show his face before the dead man's spirit. At the time, Asa said, she had the impression Hōsen was asking her to go, not because he wanted to apologize to Keigaku for all the trouble he had caused, but because of the loneliness he felt now that his old friend had died.

"I think he really lost confidence after we moved up here into the mountains. Until then, he had resented Master Keigaku, though he had no reason to do so. He used to talk all kinds of rubbish when he drank, about how he could paint just as well if he set his mind to it, he had been the better painter when they were younger, he'd had more talent, but at some point after we moved up here he started talking differently. 'It's true,' he'd say, 'Keigaku is a master, he's got amazing talent.'"

So said Asa. It seems she didn't attend Keigaku's funeral in Kyoto, but that was neither here nor there; what mattered to me was the image of Hōsen making his way to this village on the day he read of Keigaku's death in the newspaper, treading the same narrow, twisty path I had taken earlier, just below the ridge, on his way to visit the wife who had abandoned him. His figure rose before my eyes with a peculiar clarity, very small, set against the magnificent fields of short bamboo that covered the mountain slope, the late autumn wind gusting over the leaves. Later, it struck me that since Keigaku had died on the day of the Doll's Festival, on March 3, the path would still have been buried in snow; Hōsen, wearing straw sandals, perhaps, must have struggled through the drifts, and taken a very long time to get here.

At any rate, realizing that Hōsen had experienced such a day late in his life made me feel as if a single ray of white light, however faint, had pierced the dark, monochromatic vision I had created of the man, without even realizing that I was doing it.

When Asa had nothing more to say about Keigaku, I found a roundabout way, impolite as it was, to ask what had made her leave Hōsen.

And so she began: "This isn't the sort of thing you would have any experience with, I'm sure, but the truth is it's extremely unpleasant working with gunpowder in winter."

The desire to leave Hōsen had come over her quite suddenly, it seems, after they moved up into the mountains and he started playing around with gunpowder. Occasionally he would ask her to help, but that wasn't what she minded—it was how they earned their living, after all. What she detested was the way Hōsen got when he was doing that kind of work.

"When he produced his first forgeries of Keigaku's works, he did it in secret, without telling me," she went on. "Eventually he took to doing it out in the open, but I suppose early on even he was too ashamed to let me know, so he tried hard to keep it from me, to do it so I wouldn't notice. When he started making fireworks it was exactly the same. This time he wasn't doing anything wrong, though of course amateur fireworks are illegal... but still, he had no need to worry about what I would think, he could have done it openly, but instead he would wait for me to go out, or until after I went to sleep, and then set himself up at the edge of the veranda or someplace and start grinding his mortar and pestle and so on, as quietly as he could. I guess that's why I came to hate gunpowder so much."

Hōsen had first begun experimenting with gunpowder because the proprietor of a certain antique shop in Aioi was into making fireworks, and in the course of their dealings Hōsen had developed an interest in the art himself; by the time Asa learned about it, he was already wrapping various chemicals in paper packets of about forty grams each and igniting them to see what color flames they produced.

"Why was he so interested in fireworks, do you think?"

"You know..." Asa thought for a moment. "There was something odd about his fireworks. He was obsessed with producing a deep, rich violet color, like a Chinese bell-flower—I have no idea what gave him the idea. You get a color like that when you mix Paris green, potassium chloride and powdered amber, but it's always a little too light, not like an actual bellflower. Hōsen seems to have decided that one way or another he had to produce that exact color, just as deep, and then launch it in a chrysanthemum or something."

The time Hōsen lost three of his fingers, he was working on a falling star and he had accidentally thrust his pick into the section where he had set the blasting powder, causing a spark that blew up the gunpowder next to him. The incident itself hadn't necessarily stirred up any unpleasant feelings in Asa, but it inspired in her a sudden desire to leave Hōsen. She had been feeling somewhat irritated with him all along, ever since he began using gunpowder, but the explosion finally made her feel that desperate yearning to get away from him.

"Did he ever achieve that violet?" I asked.

"I don't know," Asa replied, sounding as if she didn't much care one way or the other. "He never seemed happy with the color, at least while I was there." I had the sense that talking about Hōsen had rekindled some of the love she had felt for him; her tone remained flat, her attitude cool and distant, but she never once spoke with real malice.

"In the end, I think he was an unhappy man. I often think about that. I ruined my life on account of him, more or less, but I think his life was even unhappier than mine. He loved painting more than three square meals, but he strayed down the wrong path and ended his life without ever creating a single painting worth anything, and then when he started doing fireworks he lost three fingers, and that violet he was always going on about, trying so hard to make—well, he probably didn't succeed there, either. It's not that he was a bad man, he was just born to live an unhappy life."

I listened to Asa's talk for more than an hour. There was something nice about the way she spoke, as if she were watching Hōsen, never taking her eyes off him, but from a great distance—or as if she had somehow contained him, the man he had been, within her. I got the feeling that in the course of nearly three decades living with Hara Hōsen, she had matured, emotionally, in a very particular way that made her unlike other women.

"Do you know a large distillery in Wake?" I asked, remembering the story about her and Hōsen going to see the company president together.

"No, I'm afraid I don't," she replied right away, as though she meant it. Maybe she didn't like talking about those days, when they were young. Or maybe, it occurred to me, the woman who had gone to the president's house had been someone else, not her... I let the topic drop.

Leaving enough time so that I wouldn't be late for my five o'clock appointment with the truck, I brought an end to this peculiar visit, in the course of which I had heard all kinds of details about a stranger's life without even being offered a cup of tea, and left the house behind.

Among the various stories Hōsen's widow had shared, I had been most intrigued by the one about his desire to launch a deep-violet chrysanthemum. At the time it hadn't struck me all that forcefully, but it lingered with an odd insistence in my heart, and I found myself recalling it at odd moments.

Once, after we had left that mountain village behind and moved to a place in the suburbs of Osaka, I happened to mention Hōsen's ambition—or, if that's too grand a word, his dream—to my wife. No sooner had I had finished than she grimaced and remarked, "How awful." The expression on her face suggested she could hardly bear the idea of such a firework.

"Why? What's so awful about it?"

"I mean... I don't know how to put it, I just don't like the thought. A big burst of violet opening against a dark sky."

Something told me I had touched an emotion better left alone, so I decided not to talk any more about Hōsen and hurriedly shifted the conversation. It was a trivial thing, it meant nothing; and yet my wife's attitude struck me with all the force of a discovery, utterly unexpected, and the impression lingered. I half understood how she felt, but when I considered it more closely I realized that in fact it really didn't make sense to me. Perhaps, I thought, whatever it was my wife found so awful was the same thing Hōsen's widow had noticed inside him that prompted her to leave. Perhaps something in all this surpassed my comprehension, something in the almost physiological revulsion that prevented women from feeling for Hōsen once he become involved with gunpowder, even one who had stood by his side for decades as he earned his livelihood by painting counterfeits.

I myself sensed, in Hōsen's experiments with gunpowder, something of the dark, cold nature of gunpowder itself. But it did not evoke in me feelings like those my wife and Hōsen's widow seem to have had. The image of a few violet flowers suddenly blossoming in a dark nighttime sky, which the counterfeiter needed more than anything else at a time when his life lay in shambles around him, struck me, indeed, as possessing a certain mournful beauty.

I doubted Hōsen's dream had ever bloomed like that against the darkness. Now that he had died, there was no way to ask. I couldn't help thinking, though, that it was precisely the impossibility of the color of those blossoms that had inspired such intense disgust in the two women.

After that, without my even noticing, Hōsen left my thoughts. It was only natural, I suppose: as time passed, the less-than-cheerful stories of a certain counterfeiter I had chanced to hear in the mountains where my family had fled the war gradually faded from my memory. But in the end, Hōsen was simply biding his time, waiting for the moment, two years after the war ended, when he could rise up before me one last time, as if to bring closure to the tale of his life as I had heard it.

It was summer. For the first time in a year and a few months I was riding the Hakubi line from Okayama to Yonago, over the Chūgoku mountains, to research an article for the Sunday edition about a comprehensive exhibition being held in one of the prefectures in the San'in region, linking it to the issue of provincial cultures. The train pulled up to the platform of the small station at the summit where, shouldering as much luggage as I could bear, I had embarked and disembarked so many times, and I saw the tall weeds that bordered it stirring in the winds sweeping the plateau, and then to the west the red cliffs, from which sand constantly spilled onto the road below, hissing faintly, and it suddenly struck me that it would cause no major difficulties if I were to arrive at my destination one train later. I hesitated for a while, debating whether or not to get off; then, just as the train was preparing to leave, I grabbed my bag from the rack and leapt down onto the platform. The period when my family had lived here being what it was, the area brimmed with all manner of painful memories of a sort I could never experience anywhere else, and, even if I couldn't make it to the village where we had stayed, I thought it might be nice to spend two hours or so here, drinking in the familiar scenery of the square in front of the station, the houses in the village. If I didn't jump down now, I would probably never have another chance to get off at this station.

I walked out the gate, wondering if I would bump into anyone I knew, then decided to take a rest and headed for the village's only restaurant, opposite the station. All of a sudden someone called out behind me in the accent peculiar to the region.

"Hey, aren't you the guy from the Youth Center?"

Looking back, I realized it was a young man who had chopped firewood for us and was known by the nickname "Uranbe," the second son at the farm next to the school.

I chatted with the young man for a while. He told me, in a somewhat Reddish tone typical of the time, that before long the exploitation of the farmers would start up again. He never once asked after my family, never mentioned any of the other villagers; I sensed the baffled fury at the age that burned in his breast, and in the breasts of the other young men in these mountains.

"Going up to the village?" he asked.

When I replied that I didn't have enough time today and asked him to say hello to people, he told me five villages had organized the first fireworks display since the war that evening, and if I could wait two hours lots of folks from the village would be coming to watch—it wasn't long, why not stick around? So I decided to delay my departure by two trains instead of one. If it meant I'd see the villagers, I wanted to stay and thank them for all the help they had given us when we lived here.

I passed the two hours from three to five in the station's waiting room and in the restaurant across the square. The utility poles in the square were plastered with posters announcing the fireworks, the writing done, I was sure, by young men from the area—the red calligraphy, bleeding into the paper, was truly terrible. At five, though it was still a little early, I headed for the spot where the young man said the fireworks would be launched, which was part of an enormous field about five or six hundred meters northeast of the station. There was a small river, perhaps four meters across, the embankment of which was the only location in the area suitable for launching fireworks. It was indeed a good place for fireworks; no one would be in any danger here.

A dozen or so fireworks shells, each slightly under a meter high, had been lined up like so many earthenware pipes in the clearing, which was awash with summer grasses. The sight of them poking up above the weeds gave me the strange illusion that I was looking not at fireworks, but at stupas, each one the marker for a grave. Five or six young men were sitting nearby, a boisterous gaggle of children around them. And then I ran into a man I knew from the village. He told me that maybe a hundred meters away, up on the embankment, they had a single set piece ready to go—this was the big draw tonight—and the spectators were supposed to gather beneath the railway bridge a hundred meters up from there. The villagers were sure to be along soon, too.

It must have been too early, though, because no one was around. The sun was still fairly high in the sky, up above the iron bridge.

"Five villages collaborated on the display, it's true, but ours is the only one involved in the launch," the man told me. "Used to be an old guy named Hara who made fireworks, and the youngsters learned it from him."

I hadn't realized until then that all the young men were from our village.

"Hara Hōsen, you mean," I said.

"You sure know at lot," the man said, taken aback.

"Do you think anyone here might have been close to him?"

"Well, I knew him myself, of course… There's a fellow we call Tassan, though, I guess you might say he was Old Hara's apprentice, learning to make fireworks."

The man led me over to this fellow, Tassan, who was in his forties. I didn't remember seeing him before. I asked why, and it turned out I wouldn't have because he had been in the military throughout the war and had only been repatriated from the Soviet Union late last year. He had an extremely gruff, even angry tone, but I didn't get the impression, as we talked, that he was such an unpleasant fellow, and while words didn't come easily to him he was talkative enough. Evidently he was supervising the display that evening, and as the need arose he kept issuing orders to the young men around him.

"Old Hara's fireworks... Well, he was just an amateur, of course, since he got into it as a hobby, but if you ask me he had a real talent for rapid fire. Naturally, I don't know how people do it in the cities," Tassan said. Then, pausing to chase off the children who had clustered around, he called out to the young men, "All right, let's send up two or three, get 'em energized."

This was the first time I had ever seen fireworks being launched. One of the young men tossed a small paper packet of gunpowder into one of the tubes, then put in the shell. He held a slow-burning fuse to the tip of a hardened chunk of gunpowder that he then tore off and chucked down into the tube. Immediately a burst of white smoke shot up into the still-sunlit sky, and there was a thunderous boom. I was stunned at how primitive the process was.

"I heard Mr. Hara was eager to make fireworks of a deep-violet color. Do you know anything about that?" I asked Tassan after the third firework, all sound and no fire, had gone up into the air.

"No, don't know about that. Actually, now that you mention it maybe I did hear something along those lines, but my memory isn't real clear," he said. Then, after a moment, "The one thing I'll never forget is the old man's last display."

When Tassan went back home the night Hara Hōsen sent up his last fireworks, he found a notice waiting for him saying he had been called up; from the time he enlisted until his return toward the end of the previous year, he had spent more than six years overseas. Presumably the special circumstances had imbued his memory of Hōsen's fireworks that night with equally special emotions.

Tassan had been in north China less than a month when he got a letter from a friend informing him of Hara Hōsen's death, mixed in among his first packet of letters from home, which reached him at his garrison in Fengtai.

"It's funny, when I heard Old Hara had died, I felt this weird sense of pity for the man. I'd never seen him that way before, but it struck me that all along he had been dying. Looking back, I got the feeling things hadn't been right with him when he did those fireworks."

"Things hadn't been right?"

"Sounds strange to put it like that, I know," Tassan said. "It was just something about the way he looked that night—I can't forget it, even now."

Hōsen's last fireworks display was part of a celebration of the two thousand six hundredth year of the imperial calendar or some such thing, and it was sponsored by a few neighboring villages, like the one that evening; it was held on the grounds of an elementary school in a village two stations down the line toward Yonago. Since no one else in the area knew anything about fireworks back then, Hōsen had agreed to handle the display; for two months prior to the event he worked to prepare the shells with young men from the village, and then he went to the site and launched them himself.

"We were just amateurs, of course, so there wasn't much to the fireworks, but the rapid firing sure was remarkable." I could tell Tassan was still proud of that display, so many years ago.

They had prepared sixty-four twelve-centimeter chrysanthemum shells for the event; Tassan was responsible for passing them to Hōsen, who tossed them into the tubes at a rate of about twenty a minute.

"When you're doing rapid fire, you try to have the next one go up just as the first one is bursting overhead—space 'em out any more and it gets dull. Thing is, it's pretty darn hard to go on chucking the shells in those tubes like that, keeping up the pace."

And that, Tassan said, was just what Hōsen had done so splendidly, even with three fingers missing. The venue wasn't a wide-open field like the one tonight: thousands of spectators were crammed into a plot next to the school, sandwiched between the town hall and the road, creating an atmosphere so lively you almost never saw anything like it in this region.

Hōsen, Tassan and three or four other young men were the only ones by the launching pad, which they set up in the playground, next to the horizontal bars. In a rapid-fire display you keep tossing in one shell after the next, so almost immediately the tubes burst into bright red flames, and you have to keep changing them all the time, but Hōsen managed that, too, moving so fast you could hardly believe he was as old as he was. But after repeating the same gesture so many times, and in the same hunched posture, it was impossible for him to straighten up immediately. And so, having launched the last of the sixty chrysanthemums just as smoothly as could be, still bent over, he asked Tassan—

"How was it? Was it beautiful?"

He had been too busy launching the fireworks to look up.

When Tassan told him they had been magnificent, he plopped down on the ground, his back still curved, and sat with his head down, saying nothing, panting loudly from an exertion that seemed to have sapped the sixty-seven-year-old man's strength.

At last, without turning to face Tassan, he spoke. "I heard a lot of ooing and aahing."

Tassan had been in such a dream-like state until a moment ago, as he was passing the shells along to Hōsen, that he hadn't even noticed the cheers rising from the crowd; the sound came to him only now that Hōsen had mentioned it. Hōsen, too, must have been in that same hazy state, and heard the cheering for the first time as an echo, coming faintly to life inside him, once the display was over.

Tassan had told me how deeply Hōsen had impressed him that night; hearing the story, I found myself picturing the old man then, and the vision touched a chord in me, too. I took out my cigarettes and held them out to Tassan. He thanked me, took one, and slipped it in its shirt pocket.

"No smoking here," he said.

Stupid of me, I thought, and hurriedly put them away.

"Seven years now, isn't it, since Hōsen died?" I asked.

"That's right. I was thirty-four when I got called up, now I'm forty." Tassan smiled in an offhand manner. "The old man, he—" he began, then stopped. Soon he remarked that the villagers should be turning up any time now. Turning toward the bridge, I saw that it was true: little by little, a crowd was gathering as people ambled in groups of three or five along the raised paths that cut across the fields, or made their way along the train tracks. Looking closer, I realized that they were moving very slowly, weighed down by mats of straw or rushes that they had brought to spread on the ground, and bundles of food and drink wrapped in *furoshiki*; only the children were darting on ahead.

The old man, he… Tassan left the thought unfinished, and I said goodbye to him and made my way along the embankment that jutted up over the narrow river toward the bridge, to see for the first time in ages whoever had come from the village where my family had taken shelter. At some point the sun had begun dropping behind the squat hills that ended in red cliffs at the western edge of the plateau; arrows of red evening light flew across the even field ahead of me, almost perfectly level.

I had the feeling I knew what Tassan had been about to say, even without hearing it. Just as Hōsen's widow and my wife had interpreted something inside him in the same way, and felt the same revulsion, Tassan and I—we two, at least—felt the same attraction when we thought of Hōsen on the night he launched his last fireworks, even if we couldn't explain what it was that made us feel that way.

I mulled this over as I walked.

*

And with that, I have set down what I know of the counter-feiter Hara Hōsen. Nothing but fragmentary stories heard from others. And yet, somewhere along the way, as I strung these pieces together, I had come to hold in my mind an image of this counterfeiter's sixty-seven-year life as a sort of flow—a dark and frigid stream. There was no rhyme or rhythm to that painful surging, the dark and turbid motion of some essence the man known as Hara Hōsen carried within him from the moment of his birth that rendered it impossible for him to live otherwise than he did. Painful, yes, but the pain was matched by the peculiar sadness of our karma, so that whenever I found myself reflecting upon the sorrows of human life I would remember that thin, swarthy man with his weak and gloomy air—this was how I imagined Hara Hōsen now—softly drawing his counterfeiter's brush across a sheet of paper, hiding what he was doing from his wife, or slipping out so she wouldn't find him twisting gunpowder up in pieces of paper and setting them on fire.

When I discovered Hōsen in the only surviving piece of writing in Keigaku's own hand, however, I felt an entirely different emotion. To think that Keigaku, the greatest painter of his age, and Hōsen, who never saw the fireworks he himself had launched and always had his back to the cheering crowds, had begun their lives at precisely the same place—the irony of it! When this fact was brought home to me, I saw Hōsen's life for the first time not as a dark, turbid stream that issued from something he had carried with him into the world, but as the tragedy of an ordinary, unremarkable man who ground himself down when the burden of his encounter with a genius proved too heavy to bear. The gloomy, fatalistic impression the counterfeiter's life had left faded away, and Hara Hōsen rose up before me in a new light, colored by a more human tragedy.

If Hara Hōsen had never been friends with Ōnuki Keigaku, if the two men had not been so close, perhaps Hōsen's life would have turned out very differently. Maybe eventually he would have entered the painting world and made enough of a name for himself that we would have remembered him, or half remembered him, as a peripheral figure awarded non-vetted status at the government exhibitions. For some reason, I can't help feeling that Keigaku played an outsize role in the misfortunes of Hōsen's life, though I may simply be reading too much into things. I wonder.

If we might envision Keigaku at the turn of the century, around the thirtieth year of the Meiji era—around the time, in other words, that he wrote his diary—as a dragon blessed with a sky full of clouds, forming a path to the heavens, Hōsen was a helpless grub who could only fall over when the mighty blast of that dragon's glory fell upon him.

When Keigaku came with his silver medal to drink with Hōsen, then a young man in his twenties, how did Hōsen sit with him? In what attitude? What was the expression on his face when he returned home and saw Keigaku's magnificently free-wheeling calligraphy on the door to his room?

Already, between 1897 and summer 1899, this man, with his small eyes, timid and yet betraying a fiercely competitive streak; his sunken cheeks and thin lips, which had a nervous, jealous air; the skin that grew progressively more spotty with age; and the forehead destined to lose its hair—for this was how I had revised my vision of Hōsen's appearance—already, slowly but irrevocably, the groundwork was being laid for the tragedy of his long, dark life.

I have decided to put a stop to my investigations of Hara Hōsen, at least for now. Because I must get on with Ōnuki Keigaku's biography, turning to the energetic rush of his middle period, beginning with his masterpiece *Mt. Fuji*, which established his position within the painting world.

These past two days, during which I added nothing to the biography of Keigaku, and sat staring out at the slopes of Mt. Amagi, the red crape myrtle in the corner of the garden suddenly lost most of its blossoms, colored so that they recall an earlier age, and at the same time, just like that, the white crape myrtle burst into bloom; the summer clouds that welled up constantly over the ridge of the mountain seemed—though I may have been imagining it—to have changed into autumn clouds, gliding along so slowly you could barely tell they were moving at all. Looking at the calendar, I realized that it was indeed the first day of autumn.

It occurred to me that those two Hōsen–Keigaku counterfeits, *Birds and Flowers* and *The Fox*, were probably hanging even now in the alcoves of those two farmhouses in the village by the ridge of the Chūgoku mountains, where autumn would already be filling the air, and suddenly the sense I once had that I was in the presence of something eternal seized me again. The feeling was connected to Keigaku and Hōsen, but there was more to it than that—it was also life itself, which held within it a kernel of truth that had nothing to do with either of them. Here, it seemed to me, there was no sense in speaking of originals and counterfeits. I sat for a while, steeped in the coolly glittering light of that awareness, thinking that when autumn set in I might go up to Kyoto and drink with Ōnuki Takuhiko, and tell him of a side of Hōsen he didn't know.

REEDS

ABOUT A MONTH AGO, *A. Newspaper* ran as the lead item in its society section a lengthy article about a father who had been searching all over for his six-year-old son, who had been kidnapped, leaving no stone unturned, until he happened to hear of a child who sounded like his son living at a temple in Shiga prefecture, out in the country, and made a trip down to see him.

When I read the article, though, it turned out that the meeting had not in fact established that the father, Mr. Y., and the boy, whose name was N., were parent and child, each one looking for the other. N., who was at the center of it all, had no recollection of his childhood, so while it was ninety percent certain that he and Mr. Y. were simply a father and his son who had been subjected to the whims of destiny, there was no way to prove conclusively that this was the case. This uncertainty, I suspected, was what made the incident seem like good material for a lead story.

All anyone knew about N.'s past was that he was Japanese; that in Shōwa 25—1950—he had been sold to a bread manufacturer in Jiamusi, China; and that eventually a kindly Japanese had brought him back to Japan, where he was raised at the temple in Shiga, where the boy's benefactor had been born.

Beyond the child's age, which was exactly right, and the strong resemblance between their features and builds, Mr. Y.'s reasons for supposing the boy was his own included three fragmentary memories that the boy had held on to despite losing the rest of his past, and each of them was quite persuasive. First, he remembered that there had been train tracks near the house he lived in when he was small; second, he recalled being on a boat that capsized, though he couldn't say when or where; and third, he knew his father's uniform had a black hat with a visor.

The father had facts to back up each of the boy's little memories. The house in Gunma prefecture where they had lived during the war had indeed been close to train tracks, and once, when they were riding a water chute during a picnic at Toshimaen, their toboggan had flipped over. And at one time in his life, when he was chief of the local station in the Shitaya Fire Brigade, Mr. Y. had worn a black hat with a visor.

Evidently Mr. Y. felt this slight amount of information was insufficient to prove that N. was really his child, but the article concluded with a quote to the effect that he planned to take charge of the boy and raise him from now on, whether or not he was the right child.

As I read this article, a scene rose up in my mind's eye of a father and a boy sitting together in a room in a temple lit by soft winter sunlight, each holding a fan of cards, concentrating on a game of picture-matching.

The boy had lost most of his cards somewhere—he had only three. He picked out one of them and laid it on the table. The father stared at the card for a long moment, then plucked a card from his own full hand and laid it down beside the boy's. For a few seconds, four eyes lingered on the faces of the two cards, trying to determine whether they made up part of the same picture.

Soon, the boy took another card from his hand. And the father began searching his hand for the card that matched it.

They wanted to create a picture of events in a past they had shared, but the fact that the boy had only three cards made this tricky. The boy's cards might show a large elephant ear—maybe not even the whole ear, but just a part; or the very bottom of the animal's foot. Picture-matching is supposed to be a game, but for Mr. Y. and N. it was a good deal more serious than that. They had to figure out, in this manner, whether or not they were father and son, related by blood.

In N.'s case, an extraordinary disruption of his life had stolen his memory, leaving him only those three cards, but to some extent we are all in this position: each of us holds one or two cards that have been in our hands for years, who knows why, while the cards that should be paired with them have disappeared, instilling in us the desire to try and learn, through our own games of picture-matching, which particular section of what larger design they might make up.

I myself have forgotten the greater part of my child-hood memories in the course of living, and yet a few small, fragmentary recollections remain vividly etched in my mind. They all date from the years before I entered elementary school, and it is impossible for me to say now which part of what picture they compose.

I must have been about five or six when this happened. My grandmother Kano and I were on the beach of a little fishing village near Shimoda, at the tip of the Izu peninsula, watching a ceremony for the launching of a newly built boat.

I'm sure it was autumn—September or October. I was neither hot nor cold, not even sitting there on the sand with my legs stretched out in front of me. Before us there was a small inlet the shape of a drawstring pouch, in the dead center of which a boat with perhaps a ten-horsepower motor floated, completely covered with flags. Years later I saw a launching ceremony for another small fishing boat at a fishing village in Wakasa where I had gone to swim: the flags had vertical stripes in five colors—white, red, purple, pink and yellow—and were hung in close succession not only from two bamboo poles, one each at the bow and stern, but also from cords strung between the poles. The ceremony for the boat my grandmother and I saw was undoubtedly more or less the same.

I stared and stared at that little boat decked out with all the flags as my grandmother watched beside me. There were crowds of men on board, but either the drinking had already ended or they were so worn out from celebrating that they were taking a break, because the fully dressed boat simply stayed where it was, bobbing there in the middle of the inlet, exuding an oddly quiet atmosphere.

We must have been waiting for someone. The village was my grandmother Kano's hometown—though of course I am basing this on knowledge I acquired later. Kano was a geisha in Shimoda when my great-grandfather took her as his mistress; after his death she was entered into our family registry as my grandmother, and I grew up in her care, but since she had been his mistress, and was inherently strong-willed, neither my family, nor the villagers, nor her relatives in her hometown liked her.

My grandmother must have been past sixty then. What had prompted that visit to the fishing village where she was born and raised, on the other side of Mt. Amagi? I'm unable to say, because I know nothing of her life in those days—but in any event there we were on the beach, facing the inlet where the newly launched boat floated, waiting for whoever was supposed to come and meet us.

Maybe my grandmother was expecting a childhood friend, now an old woman, or a niece or nephew. All I remember is us sitting on the sand, and the time we passed there, undoubtedly waiting for someone.

I suspect the reason I have never forgotten this picture, in which I myself appear, is that it seems so cheerful and relaxed, and yet at the same time feels oddly empty.

Even now, when I think of my grandmother, something in my memory of her then troubles me. Why did she make that trip to her hometown, which she had visited so infrequently before, and go out to the beach, of all places, and sit on the sand?

If there is anyone out there who can furnish some other part of this picture, I would love to place that person's card beside my own. But I doubt anyone like that is still alive.

I incorporated this little fragment of memory into a story of mine. In the story, my grandmother decides on a whim to visit the village of her birth, and she goes there, stopping by the temple on the mountainside to request prayers for the dead of the family into which she was born, and then she takes the road straight through the village, where no one recognizes her, and for the first time in ages goes out to the beach where she played every day as a child. On the strand, she sees a newly launched boat floating in the center of the inlet. This, more or less, was how I presented the episode.

Naturally, having no basis for imagining whom my grandmother might have been waiting for there on the beach, I passed over that point in silence. And so my grand-mother comes across in the story as a solitary old woman, afflicted with the prosaic loneliness of the old.

In my memory, though, my grandmother does not seem at all lonely or sad. The only feeling she evokes as she sits on the sand gazing out at the ocean is an inexplicable emptiness. She sits there even now in my memory, a look on her face that seems to be saying that the place to which old age carries us is neither a loneliness nor a sadness, but an inlet where a motorized boat in full dress floats quietly on the water.

*

I remember another fragment. This one is of a summer night. Stars were scattered across the sky. My mother and I had been standing for quite some time in a secluded, dark spot behind the train station. A wooden fence stretched on and on beside us; from time to time, we heard trains sending up puffs of steam.

My mother hadn't said a word to me the whole evening. She stood clutching a sizable bundle, tied up in a *furoshiki*, and seemed not to be thinking of me at all. I hated having to stay this long in such a dark and desolate place; I would hover for a while near my mother, then crouch down on the ground. Whenever I made to walk away, my mother would give my head a poke. She was a gentle person, and the harshness of the gesture was unlike her.

At some point, as we were standing there, my father turned up. He stood talking in a hushed tone with my mother without casting a glance in my direction. Eventually he noticed that I was there and came over, suddenly sweeping me up in his arms and hoisting me high into the air. He set me down again after that, giving my head a perfunctory rub, and then went back to my mother.

My parents talked again for a while in an undertone, and then, as though they had forgotten that I even existed, started walking together, just the two of them, down the dark road bordered by the fence. I hurried after so I wouldn't be left behind... And there the memory ends.

Years later, I told my parents all this and asked them to think where the station might have been, but neither of them could recall such a night. They couldn't identify the location for certain, because as a young army doctor my father had always been moving from one small city to the next, wherever his regiment was stationed. He said it had probably been Chikamatsu, since we lived near the station there; my mother said it was probably Toyohashi, where she often took the road behind the station.

In any event, I get a sense from this small memory that my parents were in the grip of some terrible sadness when it happened. Seeing as neither one of them remembers that night, however, whatever it was that had occurred must have been easy enough to forget once it had passed—too trivial, even, to merit description as an "incident."

I worked this little fragment, too, into a story, making it one of the main character's memories of her childhood. I had her interpret that evening as an embodiment of some secret her parents had shared, something they hid from everyone—a sort of hard core that they held in common, that could never be expunged from their shared past, no matter how hard they tried.

Here, too, I can't say I succeeded in capturing the meaning of that tiny memory. Without knowing where my father had been, where he had just come from, I will never be able to elucidate the sadness inherent in this isolated picture. Maybe he had left my mother and me to wait while he stopped by the pawn shop, or went to a friend's house to try and borrow some money, only to be refused. Or maybe, letting my imagination run, he had just come from a visit to someone about some unpleasant business involving him and my mother.

I can't help feeling that there was something about my parents then, as they exist in that fragment of memory, that veered far enough away from the ordinary to inscribe itself forcefully into my childish heart, even if it lasted only for the briefest of moments, and even if they themselves have forgotten it. In this instance I hold one card in my hand, but my parents have lost its pair.

Nearly all these broken-off memories of my childhood involve my parents or my grandmother, but there is one—just one—that revolves around someone who, for the longest time, I could not identify, in some situation at whose nature I could not even guess.

I can't be certain how old I was, but seeing as I had been put down on my back on the planks of the small boat we were in and covered with a short kimono of the sort women with babies wear—the baby inside, head poking out—I must have been still younger than in the other memories I described, perhaps four or five.

The boat sat at the water's edge, a spot overgrown with reeds and silver grass and the like, and the sun beat down directly overhead, making it seem very warm and bright. It was spring, most likely.

A man and woman lay a short distance away, embracing each other, and I was watching them. The man wasn't my father, and the woman wasn't my mother; it was a couple I didn't recognize. The man had stretched out on the deck; the woman, just beside him, had tucked her legs under her body and was leaning over the man, covering his upper body with her own. Their faces were touching, struck right up against each other, and I was afraid they might never come apart.

Still, from time to time the woman would turn to look at me. Each time, she would smile, stretch out a fair, uncovered arm in my direction. She would press her hand against my cheek, or lightly caress my lips, again and again, any number of times.

Then, withdrawing her arm, she would curl it around the man's neck. And once again their faces would be stuck together, as close as could be, and they would stay like that.

Apart from the anxiety I felt about them not coming apart, I felt strangely content watching their unmoving faces; I wasn't at all restless.

Once, I kicked off the short kimono that was covering me and got up. The woman gave a little cry, came away from the man to scoop me up, and then, either to protect me from the wind or to prevent me from moving any more, tightly wrapped me in the kimono and propped me up with my back against the side of the boat.

In that uncomfortable position, I looked out across the water and at the low hills on the far shore. A scattering of trees dotted the slopes. The lake seemed to narrow in that direction, forming a sort of channel; off to the right, the water fanned outward, stretching into the distance.

The whole shore was covered with thick-growing reeds and silver grass; several wooden platforms rose from the growth, one here, another there, jutting out over the water, a small boat tied up at each one. I didn't see any other people—just the lake, and the reeds and grasses on its shore, and the few hills surrounding the lake, everything shining brightly in the sun.

They left me in that position, unable to move, until I could hardly endure it anymore. The man and woman stayed with their faces crushed together; I waited and waited, but they didn't separate. This time, I felt sure their faces really had gotten stuck.

Eventually it got to be too much for me, and I burst out crying, shrieking as loudly as I could. The man got up and came and lifted me into the air. When I kept crying, he stepped down from the boat into the water, still carrying me, and began walking around the boat, splashing water into the air, presumably hoping this would amuse me. The water was quite shallow. The woman lay on her back in the boat. Once again, she stretched out her bare arms toward me.

The memory breaks off here. I have no recollection of where the two of them took me after that, or how I got home.

This fragment of memory bore no relation to anyone I knew. I had no idea where it might have taken place. For a very long time, I walked around carrying this card, having no notion of how it had found its way into my hands, without ever showing it to anyone.

For years, my memory of this time I spent with a young couple—I assume they must have been young—while they engaged in a bit of romance just sat there inside me, undisturbed; I made no attempt to look into it. I couldn't have looked into it even if I had wanted to, and in any case the meaning of this particular picture, on this one card, seemed clear enough.

When I was a student, I regarded the passions as something gloomy and depressing, like a mass of loathsome black snakes writhing about inside our bodies, but there was nothing dark or gloomy in the romantic scene between the couple in my memory, not even a sense of furtiveness. Everything about it was bright and clear, as far as I could see. The brilliance of that memory is what enabled me, even as a student, when I looked on the passions as something foul, even as I suffered night and day on their account, alternately railing against them and becoming their prisoner, to see affairs of the heart, in my own twisted way, as an element of life that I could affirm. If it weren't for this memory, I'm sure that during a certain period in my life I would have been more dismally scarred than I was, and suffered more, from my encounters with such feelings.

I found myself driving along the shore of the long, irregularly shaped Lake Kitakata on my way from Daishōji, in the Hokuriku region, to Fukui prefecture in the spring of Shōwa 24—or 1949, the year after the great earthquake there. I was working for an Osaka newspaper at the time, and was making the rounds of a few cities in the region—Komatsu and Daishōji and so on—preparing a series of articles about the progression of the recovery a year after the quake.

We entered the village of Yoshizaki and turned by the temple known for an old mask a woman is said to have worn long ago to frighten her daughter-in-law, and all of a sudden Lake Kitakata lay before us, small waves glittering splendidly in the sunlight all across its surface. The car crossed over to the other side at a point near the northern tip of the lake, where it narrowed to the width of a river, and from then on we drove along the right-hand shore. Low hills rose above the road on the other side, and beyond them, I had been told, was the Sea of Japan; but it didn't feel as though the ocean was so close. Here and there the earthquake had caused landslides that looked as if they could have happened yesterday.

The car drove twenty minutes along the shore of the long, narrow lake—twenty-four kilometers around, I had heard. Then, just as we were about to enter the village of Kitakata, I suddenly broke off the conversation I had been having with the driver and asked him to stop the car. All at once, it had occurred to me that the lake in that childhood memory of mine looked a lot like this. It was slightly past noon now, too, in spring, and the water was shining.

I got out of the car and stood on the shore. "Unusual for a lake to be so bright, isn't it?"

"It's only because it's spring; from fall on into winter it gets real dark here, actually—you get this feeling of solitude driving in this vicinity that I can't even describe. There's nothing else out here but this lake, after all, like a big puddle."

The driver pointed out a landslide visible on a distant hill and told me that even now some of the houses up there were still buried. I couldn't tell from the way he spoke whether the sense of solitude he had mentioned came from the landscape around the lake, or from the fact that there were houses buried under the ground. Either way, though I could see the area probably looked pretty desolate in winter and fall, just as he said, it was hard to imagine with the spring sunlight streaming down all around.

Of course, this wasn't the lake I recalled from my childhood. There were no reeds or silver grass growing on the shore, no platforms jutting out into the water where boats could be tied up.

And yet I thought the place where the man and woman had enjoyed their romance in my memory must have been very similar. The hills, the vast lake, and the brilliant sunlight were all the same.

But that lake I held in my memory was someplace I had drawn for myself, just as I pleased, over many years. I couldn't really have remembered the shore and the reeds and silver grass that grew there, even the contours of the hills, with such perfect clarity—not at that age. If I recalled anything, it was most likely the strength of the sunlight beating down onto the lake.

It didn't matter, though. The lake I had seen in my childhood must have been a lot like this. I had seen many lakes in my life, but never before had I stood on a shore this bright.

"It's dazzling," I said, repeating myself.

"You get that up in these northern provinces, I'd say," the driver said. "There's a special brightness to everything in spring up here, not just the lakes."

It occurred to me that maybe the lake I recalled had been in the northern provinces somewhere—it wasn't just the driver's words that made me think so. And now that I'd had the thought, I began to feel I was probably right about that, even if I couldn't identify which lake it had been.

And I had a reason for feeling this way, too. My father, who had graduated from Kanazawa Medical College before enrolling in the Army Medical School as a commissioned officer, lived in Kanazawa briefly, immediately after he graduated from Army School—maybe he was there doing research at his alma mater, I'm not sure—and so I, too, had spent part of my childhood there.

Two years or so passed after that drive along the shore of Lake Kitakata before I asked my mother if a maid or someone else might have taken me to a lake during our time in Kanazawa when I was little. She answered that she and my father were so young in those days they certainly weren't in any position to employ a maid. If someone had taken me to a place like that, she went on, it was probably a young woman named Mitsu, a distant relation who had left home for a time to escape some kind of trouble and came to stay with my mother.

I had always called this young woman "Aunt Omitsu," but she had died around the time I started elementary school, or maybe even earlier; she was only twenty or so. As a result, while speaking of the deceased as "Aunt Omitsu" felt perfectly natural when she came up in conversation, I had no memory of the woman herself.

About a year before she died, Aunt Omitsu had married a young official in the Forestry Bureau, which had a branch office in her village, and she left a child behind; somehow it was never entirely certain what the cause of death had been. It was an illness, of course, but after her death all kinds of rumors circulated—that she had poisoned herself, or accidentally overdosed on medicine.

"Made no end of trouble while she was alive, that girl, and stirred up more when she died."

Several times, I had heard my mother comment on her unfortunate relative in this way. And she wasn't the only one. To some extent, most of those who had known Mitsu had similar things to say when the conversation turned in her direction.

As a child, influenced by the thinking of the people around me, I had acquired a vague sense that the woman I knew as Aunt Omitsu was a bad person. The name made me think of a garishly colored moth, strewing white powder everywhere as it flew.

Two incidents explained Mitsu's bad reputation among my relatives: she had withdrawn from the girls' school she attended after some conflict about whether or not she had sent a love letter to a male student; and then, after she quit, when she was supposed to be staying at home on her best behavior, she had gotten romantically involved with Miwa, the young official in the Forestry Bureau, become pregnant with his child, and married him only after she learned that she was expecting.

Neither of these incidents was remarkable in the least—
such things happen all the time—but out in the countryside
people appear to have regarded her as an extremely lewd
woman.

During my student days, however, I came to see Mitsu
in a slightly different light. This change in perspective was
brought about because I had a few occasions, talking with
people when I went back to visit my hometown on the Izu
peninsula, to hear stories about her.

By then, almost two decades had passed since she died,
and naturally my relatives' attitudes toward her had shifted.
They started making excuses for her, commenting that she
had been too beautiful for her own good, or that in the end
she had just been too much of a child.

As I recall, I made the first adjustment to my childhood
image of Aunt Omitsu in my first year at college, when I
returned home for the Festival of the Dead. I stayed at my
uncle's house on that trip, and while I was there I heard talk
about a man named Ryōhei who had left the village and now
ran a successful business selling Western goods in Yokohama.

"I hear Ryōhei's in town," my uncle said. "How many
years has it been, I wonder? Used to come down every year
to say a prayer for Omitsu at her grave. Guess his passions
have cooled."

When I asked why he visited Aunt Omitsu's grave, my aunt jumped in.

"There's a riddle," she said, laughing. "Must have liked her, don't you think?"

"Not a riddle Ryōhei will ever solve, though, now she's dead," my uncle said.

The next day, I saw the middle-aged man they had been talking about, Ryōhei, walk past the house in a suit. He was thin with an honest air and a receding hairline; he had the composed manner, as he greeted people in the street, of a moderately successful man.

When he and Mitsu were young, there had been some discussion of their marrying—that was the extent of their relationship. There don't seem to have been any amorous goings-on between them; it was an ordinary match, arranged by a third party. In the end, for whatever reason, the discussions fell apart, and the possibility of a match between them faded.

The rumor that Ryōhei had been in love with Mitsu made its way around the village only after she got married, gave birth to her child, and left the world behind shortly after.

Ryōhei had already moved to Yokohama by then, but each July he would go home for the Festival of the Dead and pay his respects at Mitsu's grave. He never visited any of his relatives' graves, aside from his own immediate family's plot, but he made sure to go to Mitsu's before he left. This gave rise to the rumor that he had been seriously in love with her, which gradually spread.

Year after year, Ryōhei kept coming to pray at Mitsu's grave, as if he were making the trip down expressly to lend credence to those village rumors. Each time the Festival of the Dead rolled around, without fail, the villagers would start talking about him again. Evidently this continued for years.

I heard about one more incident back then, when I was in school. It seems a cousin of Mitsu's, a man by the name of Togashi Kiyoji who worked in lumber, had declared in his youth that he wanted to marry Mitsu; he ran into stiff resistance from the whole family on account of the fact that he and she were cousins, and in the end he had gone after Mitsu's older brother, who was the most vehemently opposed, chasing after him with a carving knife.

Togashi Kiyoji was a good friend of mine. Whenever I went back to my hometown, we would go out and cast nets into the river together.

Until I heard that story, I would never have believed Togashi could have such an incident in his past. He was a good man, carefree, happy-go-lucky. I couldn't imagine him ever being seized by such violent passion, even temporarily.

And then there was one more story—this one from a slightly later time, after I graduated college and joined society—about the eldest son of the owner of a very large jewelry store in Tokyo, who had made Mitsu a formal offer of marriage, relying on the services of a go-between.

On this occasion, Mitsu's father had refused, saying the families were separated by too wide a gap, and that he would be incapable of preparing adequately for the wedding.

The jeweler's son, who was enrolled at a private university in Tokyo, came down shortly after to meet with Mitsu himself, but she happened to be visiting a town several kilometers off when he arrived, so he stayed at the village inn that night and went back to the city without seeing her. Two years later, he killed himself in Tokyo. The newspapers said he'd been studying too hard for the upper civil service exam, that he suffered a nervous breakdown and poisoned himself, but it had happened almost immediately after Mitsu passed away, and people in the village assumed his death was related to hers.

Somewhere along the way, as I learned of these incidents involving Mitsu, I began little by little to amend my childhood image of Aunt Omitsu.

For someone who lived only twenty years, Mitsu certainly managed to make a lot of waves in the lives around her.

And while those involved might have disagreed, from a more neutral perspective there was something gorgeous and colorful about all those waves—something that not only failed to strike me, young man that I was then, as legitimate material to use in criticizing her, but actually gave me the impression that she was a very special woman, lovely and intriguing. She had stirred up all kinds of trouble, and then, just like that, she died. In a sense, it was almost awe-inspiring.

When my mother suggested that it might have been Mitsu who took me to the lake, the woman I had known as "Aunt Omitsu" appeared before me for the first time as a figure connected to my own life.

"Now that you mention it, she did seem quite fond of you," my mother said. "Very fair skin she had. The sort of face men fall for, I guess you could say, not really a great beauty—but things were never quiet around her, that was for sure. Must have been her personality they liked, I suppose... She seemed fond of you, though, it's true."

Knowing my mother, I suspect that—young as she was at the time—she must have been among Mitsu's strictest guardians; and yet, listening to her talk, I sensed only the faint nostalgia one feels for those who died long ago.

"When she stayed with us in Kanazawa that time—we

didn't know it, but she was carrying a child in her belly then. That was Kōnosuke."

Kōnosuke was the boy she had left behind when she died—a small, fair-skinned electrician whom I had met two or three times at family gatherings. I was slightly shocked, somehow, when my mother told me that. Because I found myself recalling the couple making love in my little snippet of memory, and it occurred to me that maybe it had some connection to Kōnosuke's birth.

But when I asked my mother whether Kōnosuke's father, Miwa, had ever come to Kanazawa, she immediately knocked that idea down.

"No, he was a mild, timid sort of man, Miwa was, and when Mitsu started getting a reputation in the village, he turned into a big coward—he wasn't in any shape to be visiting Kanazawa," she said. "Besides, Mitsu seemed to have got sick of him finally, him being the sort of man he was, and she wasn't eager to marry him. But then in the end she was pregnant, after all. She gave birth right after she left us, and went back."

"Didn't you notice she was getting big?"

"It's hard to believe we were so oblivious, but no, we didn't. I was young, of course, but I have the feeling she must have been unusually small, too." My mother chuckled, then added that maybe the baby in Mitsu's belly hadn't grown very big because his mother didn't care much for his father.

In short, Mitsu's pregnancy led her into a marriage she didn't really desire. Of course, people were pressuring them to marry, too, whether or not they wanted to.

I got the sense that the special circumstances of their marriage had something to do with Mitsu's staying with us in Kanazawa during her pregnancy, and then after her death with the spread of those nasty rumors.

Naturally, I'll never know the true location of that picture in my memory—of that shore, glowing the way it only ever could in spring—or be certain who that couple was. All I have is this single card, and I don't know who else might have another to lay down beside it, or whether such a card can even be found in this world, or if it has long since vanished without a trace. Either way, this picture alone stands out among my few fragmentary childhood memories for the clarity with which it is drawn.

Now, whenever I recall that scene, I think of it, for no good reason, as having taken place on that little lake near the Sea of Japan, Lake Kitakata, and tell myself that the people who appear in it are Aunt Omitsu and her lover, a man no one alive knows anything about. And it seems that as time goes by, this supposition is slowly being transformed in my heart into a matter of unquestionable fact.

Was her lover, the man who lifted me in his arms and strode with me into the waters of the lake, someone she had met for the first time only after she came to Kanazawa?

Of course, it doesn't matter. However I imagine it, I am still only imagining.

I know the indescribable brilliance of the spring sunlight that streamed down onto the face of the lake that day. That's all. The woman in that scene may have carried a tiny life inside her; that has no bearing on the picture's meaning, none at all. It does not make her lewd, or self-indulgent.

Sometimes, the twenty brief years of Mitsu's life appear to me to have possessed an extraordinary breadth. It happens when I think of her bare, fair-skinned arms reaching out in my direction, and the water sparkling behind them. But I don't know what makes me feel that way.

MR. GOODALL'S GLOVES

THIS AUTUMN, in the course of a trip down to Kyūshū to take care of some business, I set foot for the first time in Nagasaki, a city I had never before had the good fortune to visit, and in the course of my stay I happened upon certain objects that reminded me of two figures who lived in the Meiji period, both of whom have some connection to my own life.

The first was a sample of Matsumoto Jun's calligraphy. The evening I arrived in Nagasaki, a friend invited me to K., an expensive restaurant notable as one of the venues where "men of high purpose" gathered and made merry during the Restoration. Worn out from traveling, I would have preferred to take it easy at the inn where I was staying, but it seemed heartless to reject the hospitality of a friend I had not seen in years; and so, in the end, I did go to the restaurant, which was tucked away in a corner of an entertainment district called Maruyama that has been built on the mountainside, on a rather steep slope, and is evidently classified as one of Nagasaki's historic sites.

Hearing that the place had been favored by Restoration-era patriots called up images of the rowdy tumultuousness that took hold of similarly luxurious establishments across the country during the war, as commissioned officers in the army and navy claimed them for their own private use, behaving as they pleased, with no regard for anyone else, and these memories made me somewhat hesitant to visit such a place. Once I stepped through the old-style entryway, though, with its two hanging lanterns outside, each so big I could barely have put my arms around it, and the great buckets of water lined up along the wall in case of fire, I felt a kind of nostalgia for the dreams of old warriors whose traces lingered here, and since the architecture was in the style of an earlier era of which few examples remain in Japan in this day and age, I decided that it was, after all, worth having a look.

Partway down a long, winding hall my friend and I were offered straw sandals to wear and taken out to see the spacious garden; after that, we were shown to the large room on the second floor where the patriots had had their gatherings.

According to the explanation we were given by a middle-aged woman who could have been either the pro-prietress or the head serving woman, Takasugi Shinsaku, Sakamoto Ryōma and various others had come here to enjoy themselves, to plot against the shogunate, and to plan their "Naval Auxiliary Force." Gesturing at a spot on the pillar in the alcove, she informed us that we could see gashes there that Sakamoto Ryōma had left during a sword dance. It was true: the old pillar, made from mulberry or some similar wood, bore two scars that looked to have been made by a sword.

A scroll by Rai San'yō hung in the alcove. And just to the side of the alcove, leaning outward from the transom, was a horizontal frame holding a work of calligraphy large enough to suit the spacious room. I gazed up at the piece, assuming it must have been done by another of the patriots, only to find that the four thick characters, which read "Compose on the flowers, sing of the moon," had been signed "Ranchū," and that in the square stamp under the signature I could clearly make out the name Matsumoto Jun.

That a sample of calligraphy by Ranchū, aka Matsumoto Jun, should be hanging in such a place was entirely unexpected, and it evoked a certain nostalgia in me, as though I had bumped into an old friend I had not seen in ages in some spot where I would never have thought to run into him.

Matsumoto Jun was a doctor who was active from the final decade of shogunal rule into the Meiji era, and while he was not as widely known as the old patriots, as they are called, one could not possibly tell the history of medicine in Japan without referencing his name. As it happens, my great-grandfather was one of his pupils, and the relationship between them went deeper than that of mere master and disciple; as a result, I was used to hearing his name from the time I was small.

I asked the woman who was taking us around about Matsumoto Jun, but she knew nothing at all about him. She went down to the reception area to ask how his calligraphy had come to be hanging in the room, but in the end all she could tell us was that the owners said it had been there for as long as they knew, and they had left it up because there was no particular reason to take it down; beyond that, the most they could offer was that the calligrapher had been a doctor.

Though at first the writing had felt out of place, upon reflection I realized it wasn't really all that surprising that Matsumoto Jun should have come here to enjoy himself.

Looking him up in a biographical dictionary, this is what one finds:

Matsumoto Jun; childhood name Ryōjun; pen name Ranchū. Second son of Sakura domain physician Satō Taizen. Born on the 16th of the 6th month of Tenpō 3. In Kaei 3, having been adopted as successor by shogunal physician Matsumoto

Ryōsuke, he was dispatched by the shogunate to study in Nagasaki; upon returning to Edo he opened his own school and took pupils. In Meiji 1, during the Boshin War, he was imprisoned after establishing a hospital in Aizu to tend to the Northeast Army troops; subsequently pardoned, he went on to found a hospital in Waseda, then through Lord Yamagata obtained a post in the Ministry of War, where he worked tirelessly to set up the Army Medical Division and the Army Hospital in Hanzōmon. During the Saga Rebellion, the Conquest of Taiwan, the Seinan War, and other conflicts, he presided over medical affairs from Tokyo, serving as the country's first surgeon general. The convention by which families of fallen soldiers make pledges with their own hands to send to the front is said to originate in a proposal he made to the government. In Meiji 23, Matsumoto joined the House of Peers; in Meiji 28, he became a baron. He died on March 23, Meiji 40, at the age of 76.

One can see even from this résumé of his career that as a young man he had deep ties to Nagasaki, and given the evidence, his appearance at this restaurant was probably nothing to wonder at.

*

The person who planted in my childish heart, when I was still very small, an image of Matsumoto Jun as a man more worthy of respect than anyone else in the world was the woman my great-grandfather had taken as his mistress.

From the age of six until the spring of my thirteenth year, when I was in fifth grade, I was raised by this woman, then in her mid-fifties, at our ancestral home on the Izu peninsula. I only went to live with my family, joining my parents in the city, after Grandma Kano—this was what we called her—passed away. The reason I was raised by Grandma Kano, startling as it might seem, was that after my great-grandfather and his wife Suga died, when Grandma Kano's distinctive position as a mistress no longer really mattered, she had begun living as a member of our family on funds my parents sent her; even then, however, she could never entirely shed the wariness she felt on account of the odd status she had occupied all her life, ever since she was a young woman, and so, even though two generations had passed since my great-grandfather headed the family, she thought it would be best to strengthen her position by keeping me with her as the eldest son and heir.

My parents were young then, and in the face of Grandma Kano's persistent requests they appear to have decided, in a rather offhand way, that it would make things easier anyway if she was willing to take me, and left me in her charge. In short, I was Grandma Kano's hostage.

Even as a boy, I could tell that Grandma Kano was beautiful. There was a certain severity to her features, but it was clear her looks must have been remarkable when she was young. She came from a port town on the other side of Mt. Amagi, just across from my hometown, but at the age of eighteen or nineteen she had gone up to Tokyo as a geisha and become acquainted almost immediately with my great-grandfather, Kiyoshi, who soon redeemed her; from then on, he kept her with him wherever he was employed: during his stint as family doctor to the great Egawa clan, and as the first director of the Shizuoka Prefectural Hospital system, as he moved from one city to the next, including Kakegawa, Mishima and Shizuoka. When at the age of forty poor health obliged Kiyoshi to return home and set up a practice there, she showed herself for the first time in his hometown, half openly, taking her place as my great-grandfather's second wife. She was twenty-six at the time.

From then until her death at age sixty-three, for more than three decades, she struggled constantly against the chilly reception she was given in a rural area where every aspect of life was dominated by a feudalistic morality, even when no one's mistress was involved. Clearly, then, she had a strong will. She tended conscientiously to the needs of my great-grandfather's principal wife Suga, and served all our other relatives well. Still, she appears to have acquired a reputation as a forceful, clever woman who, precisely because she was so forceful and clever, had to be carefully watched, because one could never tell what she might be plotting.

Of all the things Grandma Kano told me between my sixth and thirteenth year, during which time she and I lived on the second floor of our family's small storehouse, the main building having been rented to an official in the Forestry Bureau, only two have remained with me to the present: that my grandfather, very generous with his money, ran through cash like water; and that Matsumoto Jun was the most magnificent person, and a truly worthy man. Grandma Kano called Matsumoto Jun "Sensei." He was the only person she referred to in that way. She never once applied the term to the principal of my elementary school, not even when she addressed him. She seemed to feel that to use the same term in reference to anyone else would constitute an affront to Matsumoto Jun's dignity.

In my childish way, I liked hearing Grandma Kano praise Matsumoto Jun. She had devoted her life to my great-grandfather, and Matsumoto Jun was my great-grandfather's mentor, the man he most respected, so as far as she was concerned it was only natural that she, too, should put her faith in him, unconditionally, without reflection. Grandma Kano taught me what a beautiful thing it is to show a person respect. Whenever she talked about Matsumoto Jun, I sensed her love for my great-grandfather seeping out from within her words; it was as though she were bowing down in reverence toward the ever so distant figure of Matsumoto Jun who stood, somewhere beyond the vast ocean of her love, as an embodiment of the absolute.

This was not the only cause of her veneration of Matsumoto Jun, however.

"He was such a splendid man, you see, people found themselves bowing their heads right down in his presence, natural as could be. Men as great as him, they aren't like other people... Since your grandfather was his pupil, he always just called him by his first name, 'Kiyoshi this' and 'Kiyoshi that,' but when he spoke to me he was always very polite, calling me 'Mrs.'"

I couldn't say how many times I heard that story. When she told me about accompanying him to see the figures built from chrysanthemums or the fireworks at Ryōgoku Bridge, she always touched on Matsumoto Jun's usage of that form of address, pronouncing the word herself as if to summon the emotions she had felt at the time. In her eyes, it seemed,

Matsumoto Jun was the one person who had treated her as Kiyoshi's lifelong partner, in the truest sense, and that had moved her profoundly, cutting into her heart so deeply that she would never in all her life forget it.

"He had a fine physique, such a sense of solidity as you couldn't hope to describe, and while a man of his rank never had to worry over money, he would spend whatever came in right away. And once he had used it all up, he would turn to your great-grandpa for assistance. Your great-grandpa just loved that, and he would rush off no matter what with money to give him."

Grandma Kano would tell me any number of such stories, and then in the end she would always turn to the same topic.

"Great men outshine the rest of us in every way. Not only was he a truly outstanding doctor, but he was such a master at everything else, as a poet, a calligrapher, anything you like, that there wasn't another person in all Japan who could rival him. Your great-grandpa used to say so all the time. Take a look at those characters there—such energy!"

With that, Grandma Kano would point up at the two horizontal pieces that hung in their frames from the transom on the second floor of the storehouse, making me look even though I was still just a boy and didn't understand a thing. Each work comprised four characters: one read "Tender as the spring," and the other "Cherish a spirit of reverence and act lightly." The first was dated "Early spring, year of the metal sheep," which is to say Meiji 16, or 1883.

Grandma Kano told me she and my great-grandfather had received one of these two works when they went up to Tokyo and visited Matsumoto Jun at his estate, so she must have been a familiar face in the household around that time. Meiji 16 was two years after my great-grandfather moved back to Izu. Matsumoto Jun would have been fifty-two, my great-grandfather forty-two, and Grandma Kano twenty-eight.

Needless to say, it was owing to Matsumoto Jun's good offices that my great-grandfather became the private doctor of the Egawa clan, whose head served as the local magistrate in Nirayama, and that he became the first director of the Prefectural Hospital; thus, even after he retired to his hometown, he would go up to Tokyo a few times a year to pay his respects to his mentor, and a few times in the course of my great-grandfather's life Matsumoto Jun came down to see him in Izu. I learned later on that when Matsumoto Jun paid a visit, it was always because he needed money. We still have a dozen or so samples of his calligraphy at home, and it turns out he took up his brush to write each of these as security for a debt. Whenever my great-grandfather heard Matsumoto was coming, he would sell some of his land so that he would be ready when his mentor arrived.

Such was their relationship. Of course, after my great-grandfather's death in Meiji 30, Grandma Kano no longer had any reason to meet Matsumoto Jun, so she looked on from our small storehouse in the mountains of Izu as he became a baron and abruptly rose to prominence; then, after he passed away, she continued to feed the flames of her veneration by giving the young boy in her charge slight glimpses of his personality.

As a child, I had my own image of Matsumoto Jun. He was bold and magnanimous, but at the same time he possessed a certain seriousness that could not be violated. His skin was fair, his hair jet black; he was chubby and of average height. When I grew older, I was startled to discover how closely my image of Matsumoto Jun resembled Okakura Tenshin in his days as head of the School of Fine Arts, photographed on horseback in a kimono.

At any rate, throughout the years I lived with Grandma Kano, I had to stand before the Buddhist altar in our rooms and place my hands together in prayer twice each month. The first time was on the day of each month when my great-grandfather had died; the second, on the day Matsumoto Jun had died.

My great-grandfather's official wife died when I was seven, so I have hardly any memories of her. Judging from the stories that have been passed down—that as the daughter of a principal advisor to a daimyo she had brought a red-lacquered bath pail as part of her trousseau; that all her life, she was hopeless in the kitchen—she must have been raised in an extremely sheltered fashion and grown into a woman notable only for her retiring nature; my great-grandfather, with his intense disposition, could hardly have been expected to feel pleased with someone like that, and as a result *that woman* ended up walking into the picture as his true lifelong partner.

Suga, his principal wife, seems to have been fairly well regarded in the country, in part because people sympathized with her plight and in part out of respect for her family; meanwhile, Grandma Kano was never well liked by the villagers, even in her old age. Behind her back they called her by her given name, "Okano," adding only the familiar "O," and the mere fact that she had taken charge of me seems to have been reason enough to criticize her.

The villagers often made comments about her to me. "Oh, you poor thing! You tell that woman to stop drinking all the time and fix you something good to eat!"

The truth was that I never suffered any sort of abuse at Grandma Kano's hands. She did make it her practice to have a bit of sake every night, but she would take her time drinking just a single small bottle-full, all the while telling me stories about Tokyo, or perhaps teaching me some new character, or talking about Matsumoto Jun. Each night, I would fall asleep in her arms.

Whenever someone sent Grandma Kano a box of confections, she would set some on the altar as offerings to my great-grandfather and Matsumoto Jun, and then she would give the rest to me, since she had no taste for sweets. Every night when I went to bed, she would wrap up some snack in paper and place it next to me on the futon so that I would have it to eat in the morning, the moment I woke up. She always made sure to leave a little out for the mice, too, twisting it up in paper and putting it on the floor, a little distance away. There were a lot of mice in the storehouse, but as long as she put food out for them they would never invade our futons.

Sometimes I woke up in the middle of the night, and when I did mice would always be scampering around near my pillow. But it was just as Grandma Kano said: however wildly they might dash about, they never came in under the covers. I was never frightened; I slept with my face buried in Grandma Kano's chest. Hearing her talk about Matsumoto

Jun had convinced me that he deserved our respect more than anyone in the world, and by the same token her assurances made me believe that the mice would never, ever get inside our futon.

Whenever I got bad grades at school, Grandma Kano would go to the teachers' room to complain. Other than that, there was nothing about her that I didn't like.

The day after I saw Matsumoto Jun's calligraphy at K., the restaurant, the same friend took me to see a succession of Nagasaki's famous places and historical sites, including Suwa Shrine, Eyeglasses Bridge, Sūfuku Temple and Dejima; by the time we left Urakami Cathedral and stepped inside the foreign cemetery in Sakamoto-machi, the sunlight, which had taken on an autumnal tint all of a sudden, was less streaming than drifting down, and the day was giving way to a tranquil twilight.

Apparently there were two other foreign cemeteries, one at the foot of Mt. Inasa and the other near Urakami Cathedral, but this one had the oldest graves. The foreign cemetery didn't really feel like a cemetery; it was a cheerful place distinguished only by the particular stillness that hung in the air. And in this bright, quiet spot were rows of crosses and busts and gravestones, each set a good distance apart from the next. A few of these markers had suffered considerable damage, likely from the atomic blast—some had had chunks blown off, others had tilted over—but none of this resulted in a sense of messiness or disorder.

Feeling the first time since my arrival that I had been liberated from the crowds of tourists, I took my time examining each word on the flat surfaces of the stones, so unlike the tall narrow markers at Japanese graves. Most memorialized men and women who had lived in Japan in the early years of the Meiji period. J.M. Standard, who was born in Edinburgh and died in Nagasaki in 1854, was among the oldest I saw; most of the people there had died two decades later, in the early years of the Meiji period. My friend, who was born in Chōfu, noted down in his notebook the name of a certain William Halbeck Evans, who had died in Chōfu in 1930, at the age of seventy-one.

"I don't know a thing about this man Evans, but he died in my hometown. Next time I go back, I might just see what I can find out."

My friend's curiosity about this man struck me as a bit funny, somehow. Without exception, every gravestone bore some variation on the phrase "In sacred memory," but by now even the memories of these people had faded away, and the feelings that moved in our hearts as we faced them seemed closer to excitement than anything else.

As we strode across the grass, I peered down at the successive graves, the perimeter of each one marked by a low stone wall.

Then, in one corner of a grave somewhat narrower than the others, overwhelmed by some plant whose thick growth of small leaves was dotted with small white flowers, I stopped and lit a cigarette. The grave belonged to E. Goodall. He had died in 1889, and beneath the English letters of his name was a transcription into *kanji*. This use of characters to write the man's name was the only thing that distinguished his grave from the others.

I began repeating the name to myself after that: *Goodall, Goodall, Goodall*. Because I had the feeling it wasn't the first time I had encountered those sounds. And as I kept at it, I suddenly realized that it was the "Goodall" from "Mr. Goodall's gloves."

I had seen the big leather gloves we referred to as "Mr. Goodall's gloves" on several occasions—this, too, during the period when I lived with Grandma Kano. This was that "Goodall." Needless to say, I had no way of knowing whether the Mr. Goodall whose name was associated with the gloves was the man resting in the earth before me, but I couldn't help marveling that in these past two days, yesterday and today, I had twice encountered things that made me think of Grandma Kano.

What kind of man was Mr. Goodall? No doubt it would be possible to research the events of his life, if one were so inclined. Even having that information, though, I doubted I could confirm one way or the other whether he was the Mr. Goodall of the gloves. Grandma Kano—who may well have had some knowledge of the person whose name went with the gloves—had long since passed away; there was no one left in the world anymore, there were no clues, that might reveal whether or not the two people were one and the same.

And yet, in part because I had stumbled upon that sample of Matsumoto Jun's calligraphy just the day before, I couldn't help feeling that the Mr. Goodall resting under the gravestone was indeed the very man with whom Grandma Kano had forged a connection one day, in the course of her long life—even if it was a connection so tenuous that it hardly seemed to deserve that name.

The third and fourth characters in Mr. Goodall's name were covered over with many layers of moss, white and green, until it was barely possible to make out the writing.

"1889. What year would that be in the Meiji period?" I asked my friend, who was staring at a stone a little ways off. He stood up right away and began crooking his fingers, counting.

"Meiji 22," he said. "Funny how many people died around Meiji 20."

I think I must have seen Mr. Goodall's gloves for the first time during a major house cleaning in the year I started elementary school. Two or three young men from another branch of the family had come to help, and when they lugged our household items and furniture down from our second-floor rooms and spread it all out across the garden, someone discovered a pair of white leather gloves, wrapped in newspaper, in one of the piles. They were extremely large, and it was the first time any of us, either I or the young men, had ever set eyes on leather gloves. One after another we slipped our hands inside, but they were so loose no one could have worn them.

"Those are useless," Grandma Kano said, watching us. "Those are Mr. Goodall's gloves."

"So they're a foreigner's! I thought they were big."

Hearing that they had belonged to a foreigner, we took turns inspecting them again.

I had never heard a foreigner's name before, and I found myself painting a picture of him in my mind's eye as a pleasant, elderly man with a ruddy face. I had seen foreigners twice before. The first time it was a couple who came to stay at a hot spring in the village; the second was when the Emperor came down to hunt, and a few foreigners came along with guns on their shoulders, mixed in among the officials from the Department of the Imperial Household.

I had seen those people from a distance, so I formed my own image of Mr. Goodall by blending what I knew from those experiences with the vaguely dull, lethargic impression I got from the name.

Once I had seen Mr. Goodall's gloves, I developed a terrible yearning to have them for myself. But as generous as Grandma Kano was in all respects, for some reason she wouldn't let me have them.

She stuffed dried leaves that acted as bug repellent into each finger, all the way down into the tip; she wrapped the gloves in two, then three layers of newspaper and tied the packet up in two directions with twine; and finally she packed them away at the bottom of a Chinese chest. She treasured those gloves, I could see that.

I looked forward more than anything to the moment when I could hold Mr. Goodall's gloves in my hands during our biannual cleanings, once in spring and once in autumn.

And I wasn't the only one: soon, Mr. Goodall's gloves became famous among the village children, and on the day of the cleaning several of us would cluster around the Chinese chest when it was carried out and set down under the chinquapin in the garden.

I didn't know who Mr. Goodall was, or how his gloves had come into Grandma Kano's possession, but I never wondered or felt the slightest desire to probe; the mere fact that the foreigner's big gloves belonged to our household was enough to satisfy me, and each year when I found them still there in the Chinese chest, I felt relief that they hadn't disappeared.

The year before her death, Grandma Kano told me a sort of story—I guess you could call it that—about Mr. Goodall's gloves. She had been suffering from cataracts for a year or so, and she tried not to go out during the day because she said things flickered in bright sunlight; even just sitting near the window, she would tilt her graceful, well-proportioned face back a little and half close her eyes.

If I said something to Grandma Kano when she was like that, she wouldn't open her eyes; since she couldn't turn to look at me, she would soften her expression into something approaching a smile. The severity that must have made her so beautiful in her youth was gone then, supplanted by a girlish, innocent look that emerged from somewhere inside her. Her cheeks were pink, with a healthy sheen. I loved

135

Grandma Kano at those times, when her eyesight was bad and that benign expression came over her face the moment I said anything to her.

One day, something prompted me to ask her about Mr. Goodall's gloves.

"Mr. Goodall was a foreigner, a very large man," she said. "He must have been fully twice as big as a Japanese man. When your great-grandfather and I went along with Matsumoto Sensei to the Red Cross in Kōjimachi, the main office, he was right there behind us when we signed our names at the reception desk."

I asked her what he had looked like.

"How would I know that? It was an extraordinary day, you see—foreigners by the hundreds, and Her Majesty the Empress was there, imperial princes and princesses, ministers. Thousands of guests, there were, and to top it all off it was snowing—the crowds were so awful you could hardly move."

The girlish mildness of her expression never varied; only her mouth moved. Clearly she took pride in the fact that she had known such scenes and sights—things the villagers could never have imagined. She named a few of the princes and princesses, some ministers, but of course I was much too young to have any idea who these people were.

"I ended up having to wait for Matsumoto Sensei and your great-grandfather by the entrance, and Mr. Goodall, a man I had never in my life met before, said it was a pity I would have to wait out in the snow for two, maybe three hours, without having any of the good food inside, so he took his gloves from his pockets and told me to put them on. He lent me those gloves," Grandma Kano said.

"You didn't return them?" I asked.

"I wanted to. Afterward Matsumoto Sensei checked the guestbook at the reception desk for me, and he learned the man's name was Mr. Goodall, but there were such crowds, you know, so many of them foreigners, too, that it would have been impossible…"

From what she said, I assumed that, unable to return "Mr. Goodall's gloves" to the man she had borrowed them from, she had taken possession of them herself.

I remember the expression on Grandma Kano's face that day with more clarity than on any other. Perhaps my heart shifted that day, and I went from being a baby to being a boy. Somehow, after hearing that story, for no reason I could have pointed to, I couldn't help feeling pity for Grandma Kano on that day when Mr. Goodall lent her his gloves.

That was the extent of Grandma Kano's story about Mr. Goodall. That was it—and yet each time I have recalled it later in my life, it has struck me that she must have felt a terrible sense of loneliness as she told it, so that over time this suspicion has acquired something of the force of certainty. Perhaps I came to think this way because Grandma Kano made an impression on me as she talked then, with her eyes shut in the manner I have described, her face slightly upturned, her expression mild and her eyes clouded by cataracts, that was so completely different from other times.

What sort of event was held that day, I wonder, when Matsumoto Jun took my great-grandfather, and Grandma Kano with him, to the Red Cross? I haven't the slightest idea, and so far not knowing has caused me no inconvenience; but if the Mr. Goodall whose name was carved in *kanji* on that grave should happen to have been the same Mr. Goodall who lent his gloves to Grandma Kano, then the event must have taken place before Meiji 22, when Mr. Goodall died. No doubt with a little research I could learn what brought so many distinguished people together under a single roof—what occasion had brought Grandma Kano to the capital with my great-grandfather, expecting that she would sit beside him at his table.

Setting that question aside, I assume this was what happened: Matsumoto Jun made the necessary arrangements for my great-grandfather and Grandma Kano to go up and attend the event, but then for some reason Grandma Kano was unable to enter, and so she ended up waiting outside in the snow, wearing the big gloves Mr. Goodall had lent her out of pity, until the gathering ended and Matsumoto Jun and my great-grandfather came out again.

I found myself imagining this as, having said goodbye to the friend who had led me around all day, I was walking up to my inn, alone now, on a sloping road whose original cobblestones had been left in place only along its edges.

I could imagine various reasons why Grandma Kano would not have been permitted to join the gathering, assuming this happened sometime before Meiji 22. Back then the whole society was bound, up and down and side to side, by a code that might well have demanded she be left standing in the snow simply because she was not my great-grandfather's official wife.

In any event, Mr. Goodall's gloves seem to have stood in Grandma Kano's mind as a memento of a less than happy element of her life. The care she lavished on Mr. Goodall's gloves was a token of her gratitude to that generous foreigner, but at the same time perhaps it also marked one of the saddest incidents in her life. Just as the extraordinary, self-denying respect she showed Matsumoto Jun was a memorial to those few small pleasures that had come her way, as if they had just happened to notice that she was there, in the course of a life that probably could not be described as happy.

I spent two nights in Nagasaki, then took the bus to Shimabara, crossed from Shimabara to Misumi on a small steamboat, and set out from there for Kumamoto.

A driving rain beat down on a rough ocean between Shimabara and Misumi, so I lay in my room the whole time, and never saw the waters people say are so beautiful.

Suffering from mild seasickness, I found myself remembering those words that had been carved on the face of every gravestone in the foreign cemetery in Nagasaki: "In sacred memory." No doubt Matsumoto Jun and Mr. Goodall had both navigated lives with a scale and breadth beyond anything Grandma Kano ever knew; and yet I wondered if perhaps it was true that they had come to life in the most fiercely sacred manner precisely in Grandma Kano's memory. And Grandma Kano, in her turn, went on living, in a certain beautiful way, in my own memory. I kept thinking about that, about the nature of our relationships, as I gave myself up to the ship's great rolling.

PUSHKIN PRESS

Pushkin Press was founded in 1997, and publishes novels, essays, memoirs, children's books—everything from timeless classics to the urgent and contemporary.

This book is part of the Pushkin Collection of paperbacks, designed to be as satisfying as possible to hold and to enjoy. It is typeset in Monotype Baskerville, based on the transitional English serif typeface designed in the mid-eighteenth century by John Baskerville. It was litho-printed on Munken Premium White Paper and notch-bound by the independently owned printer TJ International in Padstow, Cornwall. The cover, with French flaps, was printed on Colorplan Pristine White paper. The paper and cover board are both acid-free and Forest Stewardship Council (FSC) certified.

Pushkin Press publishes the best writing from around the world—great stories, beautifully produced, to be read and read again.

STEFAN ZWEIG · EDGAR ALLAN POE · ISAAC BABEL
TOMÁS GONZÁLEZ · ULRICH PLENZDORF · TEFFI
VELIBOR ČOLIĆ · LOUISE DE VILMORIN · MARCEL AYMÉ
ALEXANDER PUSHKIN · MAXIM BILLER · JULIEN GRACQ
BROTHERS GRIMM · HUGO VON HOFMANNSTHAL
GEORGE SAND · PHILIPPE BEAUSSANT · IVÁN REPILA
E.T.A. HOFFMANN · ALEXANDER LERNET-HOLENIA
YASUSHI INOUE · HENRY JAMES · FRIEDRICH TORBERG
ARTHUR SCHNITZLER · ANTOINE DE SAINT-EXUPÉRY
MACHI TAWARA · GAITO GAZDANOV · HERMANN HESSE
LOUIS COUPERUS · JAN JACOB SLAUERHOFF
PAUL MORAND · MARK TWAIN · PAUL FOURNEL
ANTAL SZERB · JONA OBERSKI · MEDARDO FRAILE
HÉCTOR ABAD · PETER HANDKE · ERNST WEISS
PENELOPE DELTA · RAYMOND RADIGUET · PETR KRÁL
ITALO SVEVO · RÉGIS DEBRAY · BRUNO SCHULZ